— **Jules Verne's** —

Around the World in 80 Days

adapted and illustrated by
Rod Espinosa

visit us at
www.abdopublishing.com

Published by Red Wagon, a division of the ABDO Publishing Group, 8000 West 78th Street, Edina, Minnesota 55439. Copyright © 2008 by Abdo Consulting Group, Inc. International copyrights reserved in all countries. All rights reserved. No part of this book may be reproduced in any form without written permission from the publisher. Graphic Planet™ is a trademark and logo of Red Wagon.

Printed in the United States.

Original novel by Jules Verne
Adapted and illustrated by Rod Espinosa
Colored and lettered by Rod Espinosa
Edited by Stephanie Hedlund
Interior layout and design by Antarctic Press
Cover art by Rod Espinosa
Cover design by Neil Klinepier

Library of Congress Cataloging-in-Publication Data

Espinosa, Rod.
    Around the world in 80 days / Jules Verne ; adapted and illustrated by Rod Espinosa.
    p. cm. -- (Graphic classics)
    Includes bibliographical references.
    ISBN 978-1-60270-050-5
    1. Graphic novels. I. Verne, Jules, 1828-1905. Tour du monde en quatre-vingts jours. II. Title.

PN6727.E86A76 2008
741.5'973--dc22

                                                 2007006444

TABLE of CONTENTS

Chapter 1 The Wager of Phileas Fogg

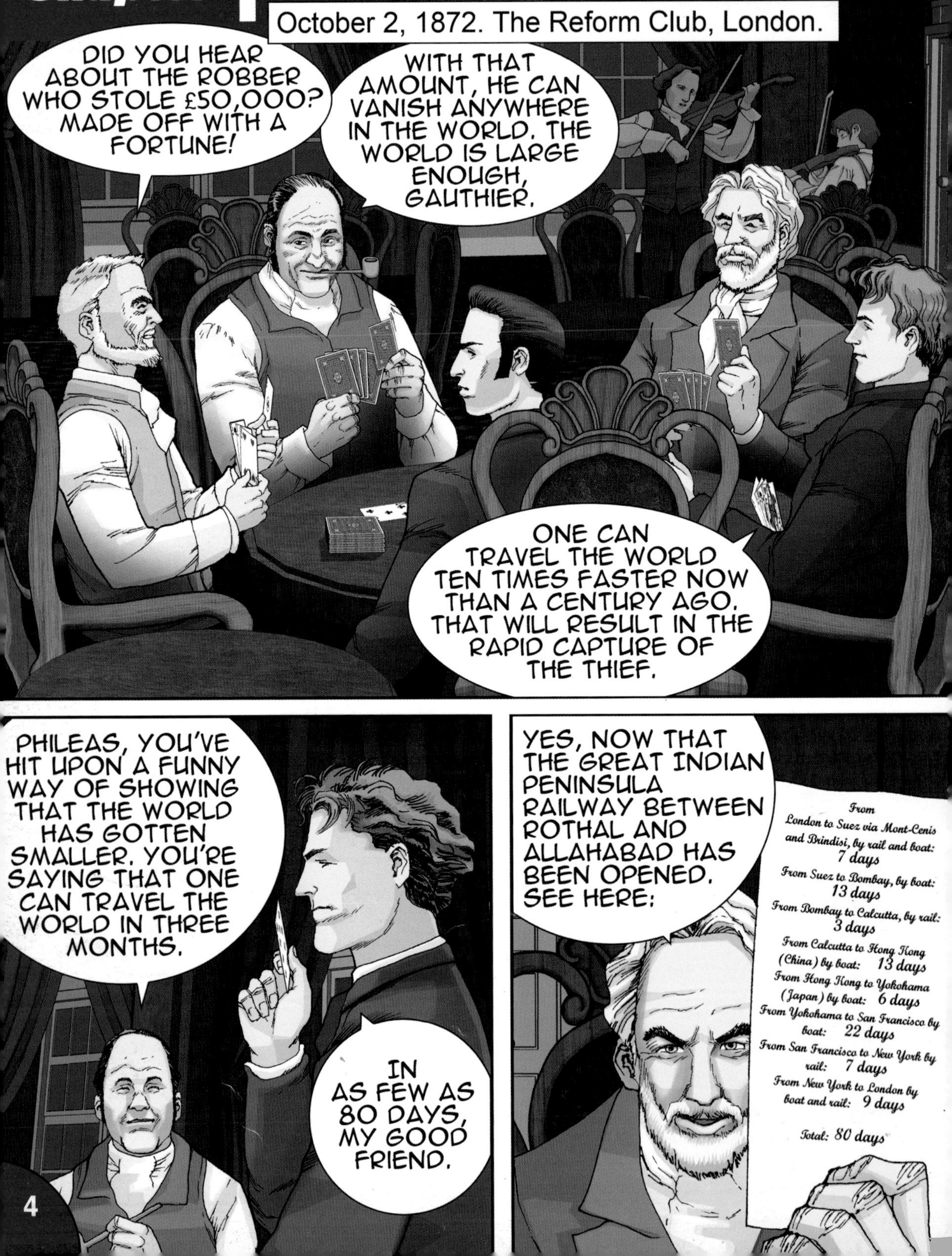

October 2, 1872. The Reform Club, London.
DID YOU HEAR ABOUT THE ROBBER WHO STOLE £50,000? MADE OFF WITH A FORTUNE!
WITH THAT AMOUNT, HE CAN VANISH ANYWHERE IN THE WORLD. THE WORLD IS LARGE ENOUGH, GAUTHIER.
ONE CAN TRAVEL THE WORLD TEN TIMES FASTER NOW THAN A CENTURY AGO. THAT WILL RESULT IN THE RAPID CAPTURE OF THE THIEF.
PHILEAS, YOU'VE HIT UPON A FUNNY WAY OF SHOWING THAT THE WORLD HAS GOTTEN SMALLER. YOU'RE SAYING THAT ONE CAN TRAVEL THE WORLD IN THREE MONTHS.
IN AS FEW AS 80 DAYS, MY GOOD FRIEND.
YES, NOW THAT THE GREAT INDIAN PENINSULA RAILWAY BETWEEN ROTHAL AND ALLAHABAD HAS BEEN OPENED. SEE HERE:
From London to Suez via Mont-Cenis and Brindisi, by rail and boat: 7 days
From Suez to Bombay, by boat: 13 days
From Bombay to Calcutta, by rail: 3 days
From Calcutta to Hong Kong (China) by boat: 13 days
From Hong Kong to Yokohama (Japan) by boat: 6 days
From Yokohama to San Francisco by boat: 22 days
From San Francisco to New York by rail: 7 days
From New York to London by boat and rail: 9 days
Total: 80 days

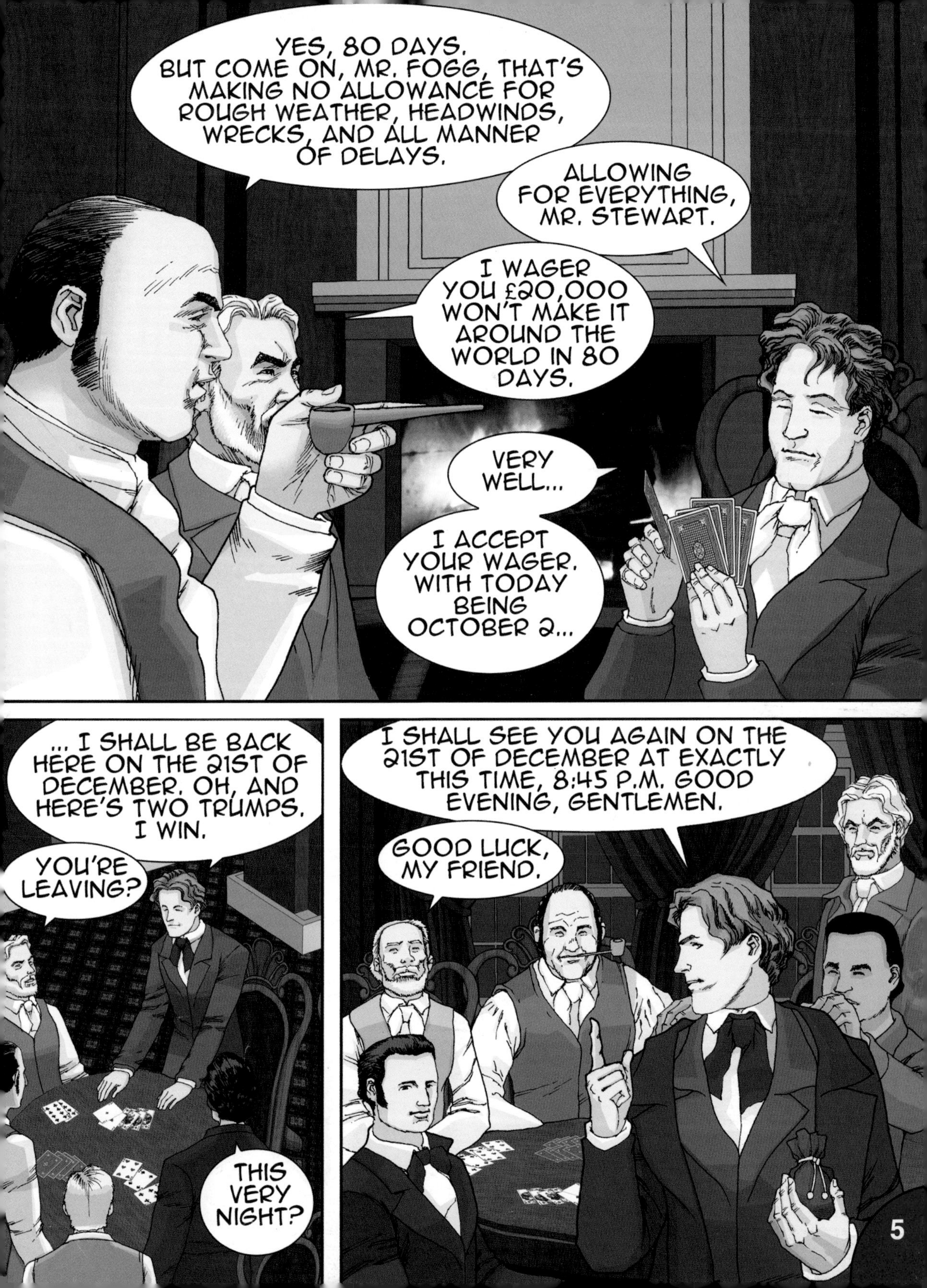
YES, 80 DAYS. BUT COME ON, MR. FOGG, THAT'S MAKING NO ALLOWANCE FOR ROUGH WEATHER, HEADWINDS, WRECKS, AND ALL MANNER OF DELAYS.
ALLOWING FOR EVERYTHING, MR. STEWART.
I WAGER YOU £20,000 WON'T MAKE IT AROUND THE WORLD IN 80 DAYS.
VERY WELL...
I ACCEPT YOUR WAGER. WITH TODAY BEING OCTOBER 2...
... I SHALL BE BACK HERE ON THE 21ST OF DECEMBER. OH, AND HERE'S TWO TRUMPS. I WIN.
YOU'RE LEAVING?
THIS VERY NIGHT?
I SHALL SEE YOU AGAIN ON THE 21ST OF DECEMBER AT EXACTLY THIS TIME, 8:45 P.M. GOOD EVENING, GENTLEMEN.
GOOD LUCK, MY FRIEND.

Chapter 2 The Journey Begins!

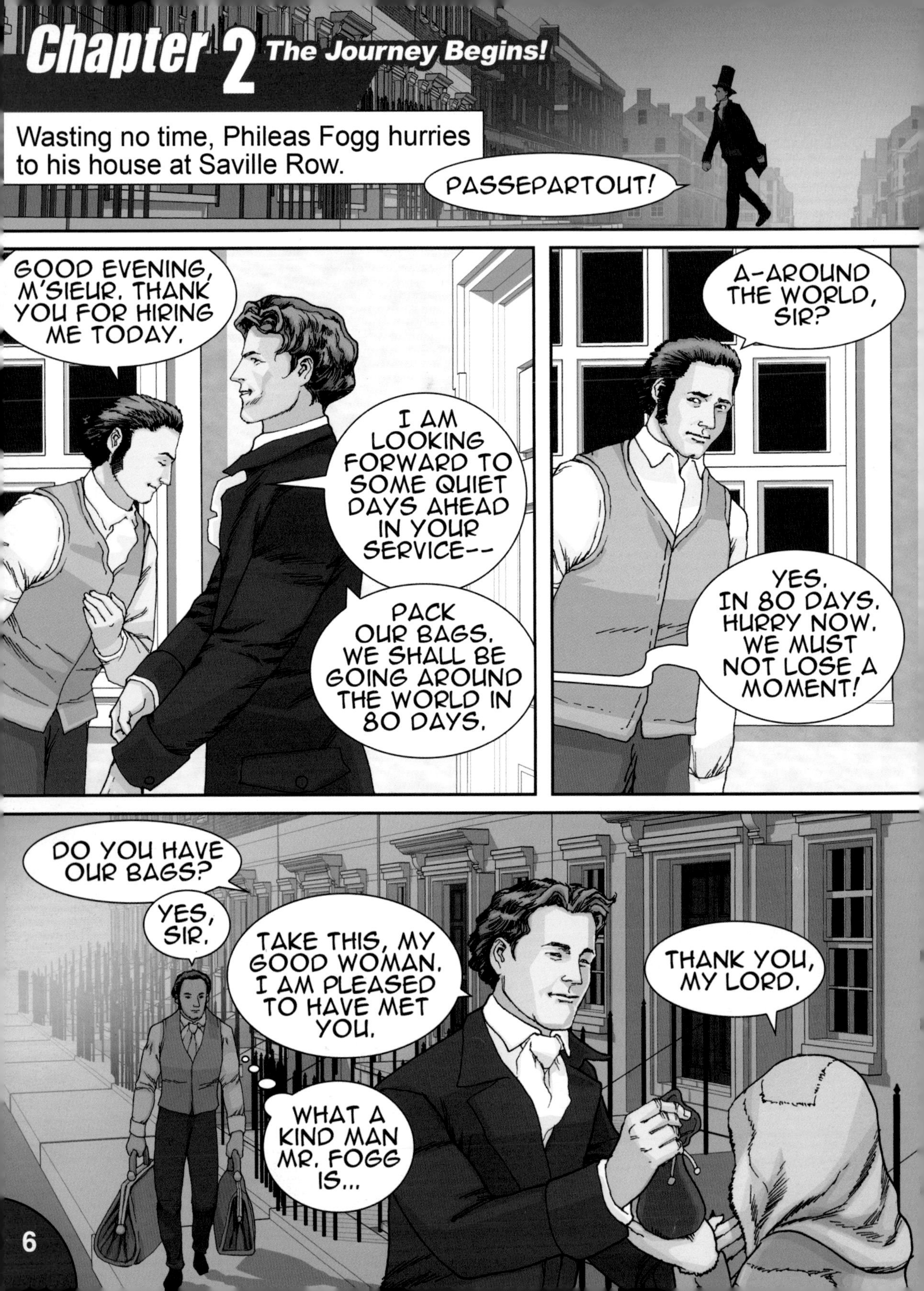
Wasting no time, Phileas Fogg hurries to his house at Saville Row.
PASSEPARTOUT!
GOOD EVENING, M'SIEUR. THANK YOU FOR HIRING ME TODAY.
I AM LOOKING FORWARD TO SOME QUIET DAYS AHEAD IN YOUR SERVICE--
PACK OUR BAGS. WE SHALL BE GOING AROUND THE WORLD IN 80 DAYS.
A-AROUND THE WORLD, SIR?
YES. IN 80 DAYS. HURRY NOW. WE MUST NOT LOSE A MOMENT!
DO YOU HAVE OUR BAGS?
YES, SIR.
TAKE THIS, MY GOOD WOMAN. I AM PLEASED TO HAVE MET YOU.
WHAT A KIND MAN MR. FOGG IS...
THANK YOU, MY LORD.

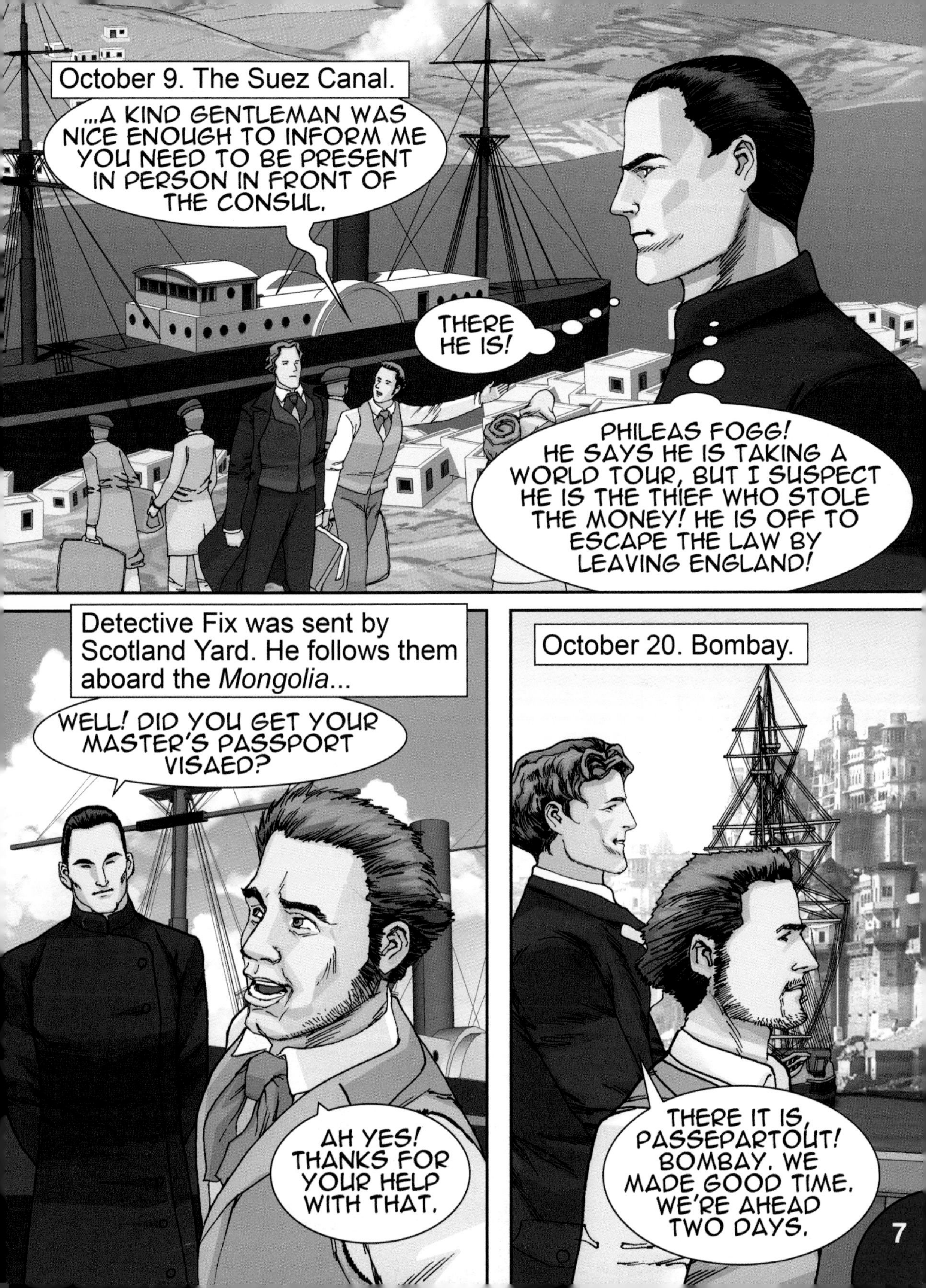
October 9. The Suez Canal.
...A KIND GENTLEMAN WAS NICE ENOUGH TO INFORM ME YOU NEED TO BE PRESENT IN PERSON IN FRONT OF THE CONSUL.
THERE HE IS!
PHILEAS FOGG! HE SAYS HE IS TAKING A WORLD TOUR, BUT I SUSPECT HE IS THE THIEF WHO STOLE THE MONEY! HE IS OFF TO ESCAPE THE LAW BY LEAVING ENGLAND!
Detective Fix was sent by Scotland Yard. He follows them aboard the *Mongolia*...
WELL! DID YOU GET YOUR MASTER'S PASSPORT VISAED?
AH YES! THANKS FOR YOUR HELP WITH THAT.
October 20. Bombay.
THERE IT IS, PASSEPARTOUT! BOMBAY. WE MADE GOOD TIME. WE'RE AHEAD TWO DAYS.

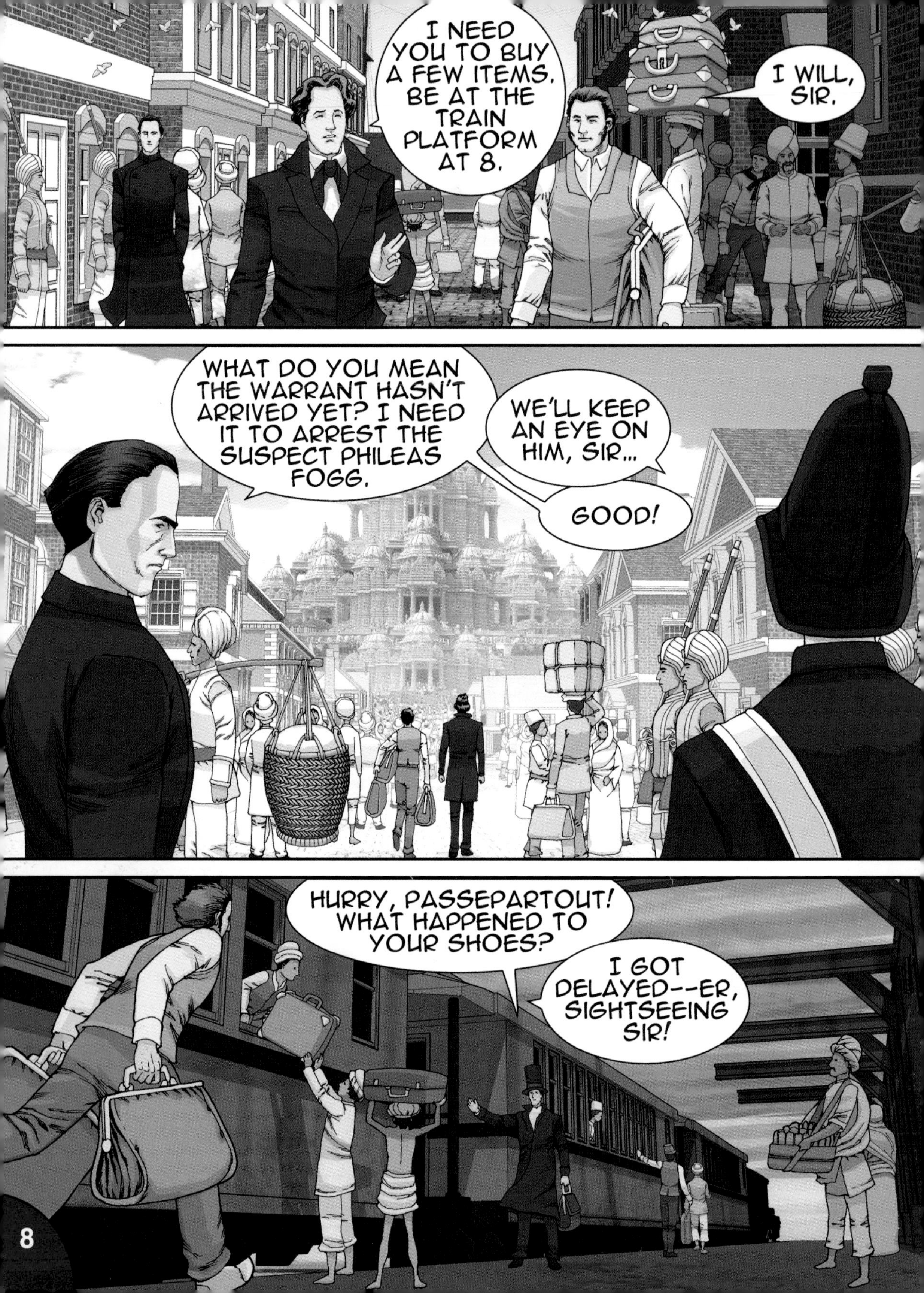
I NEED YOU TO BUY A FEW ITEMS. BE AT THE TRAIN PLATFORM AT 8.
I WILL, SIR.
WHAT DO YOU MEAN THE WARRANT HASN'T ARRIVED YET? I NEED IT TO ARREST THE SUSPECT PHILEAS FOGG.
WE'LL KEEP AN EYE ON HIM, SIR...
GOOD!
HURRY, PASSEPARTOUT! WHAT HAPPENED TO YOUR SHOES?
I GOT DELAYED--ER, SIGHTSEEING SIR!

October 21. The interior of India.

Fweeeeee!

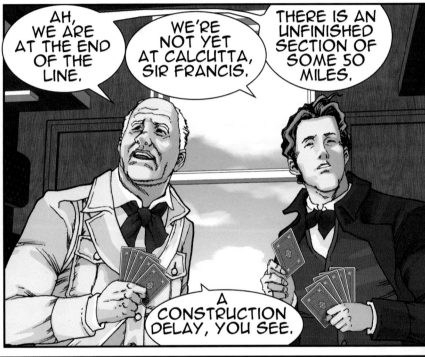

AH, WE ARE AT THE END OF THE LINE.

WE'RE NOT YET AT CALCUTTA, SIR FRANCIS.

THERE IS AN UNFINISHED SECTION OF SOME 50 MILES.

A CONSTRUCTION DELAY, YOU SEE.

WILL THIS DELAY YOUR TRIP, MR. FOGG?

NOT AT ALL, SIR FRANCIS. DELAYS LIKE THIS WERE EXPECTED.

WE SHALL WALK IF WE HAVE TO.

SIR, I HAVE ANOTHER IDEA...

9

Chapter 3 Unexpected Adventure!

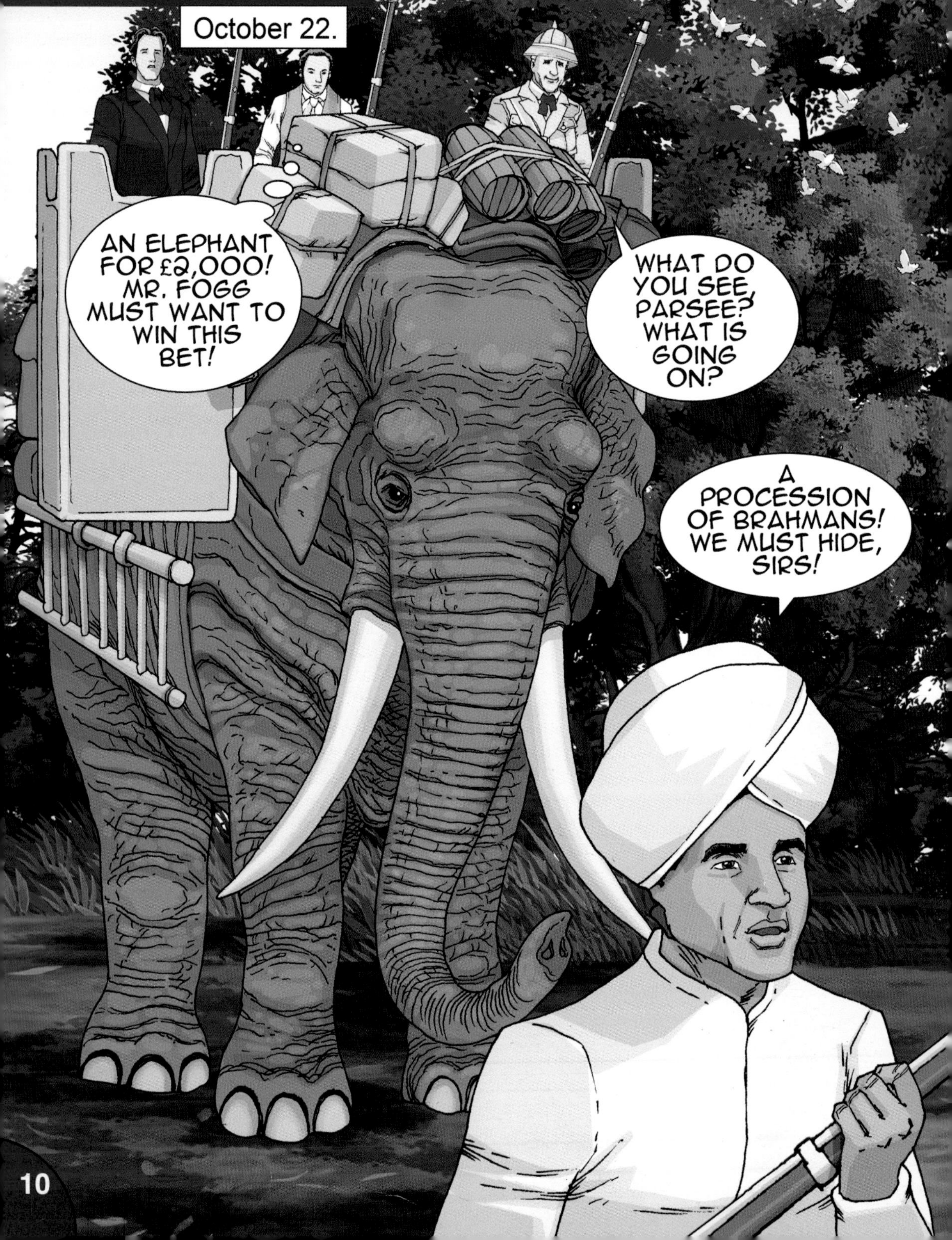
October 22.
AN ELEPHANT FOR £2,000! MR. FOGG MUST WANT TO WIN THIS BET!
WHAT DO YOU SEE, PARSEE? WHAT IS GOING ON?
A PROCESSION OF BRAHMANS! WE MUST HIDE, SIRS!

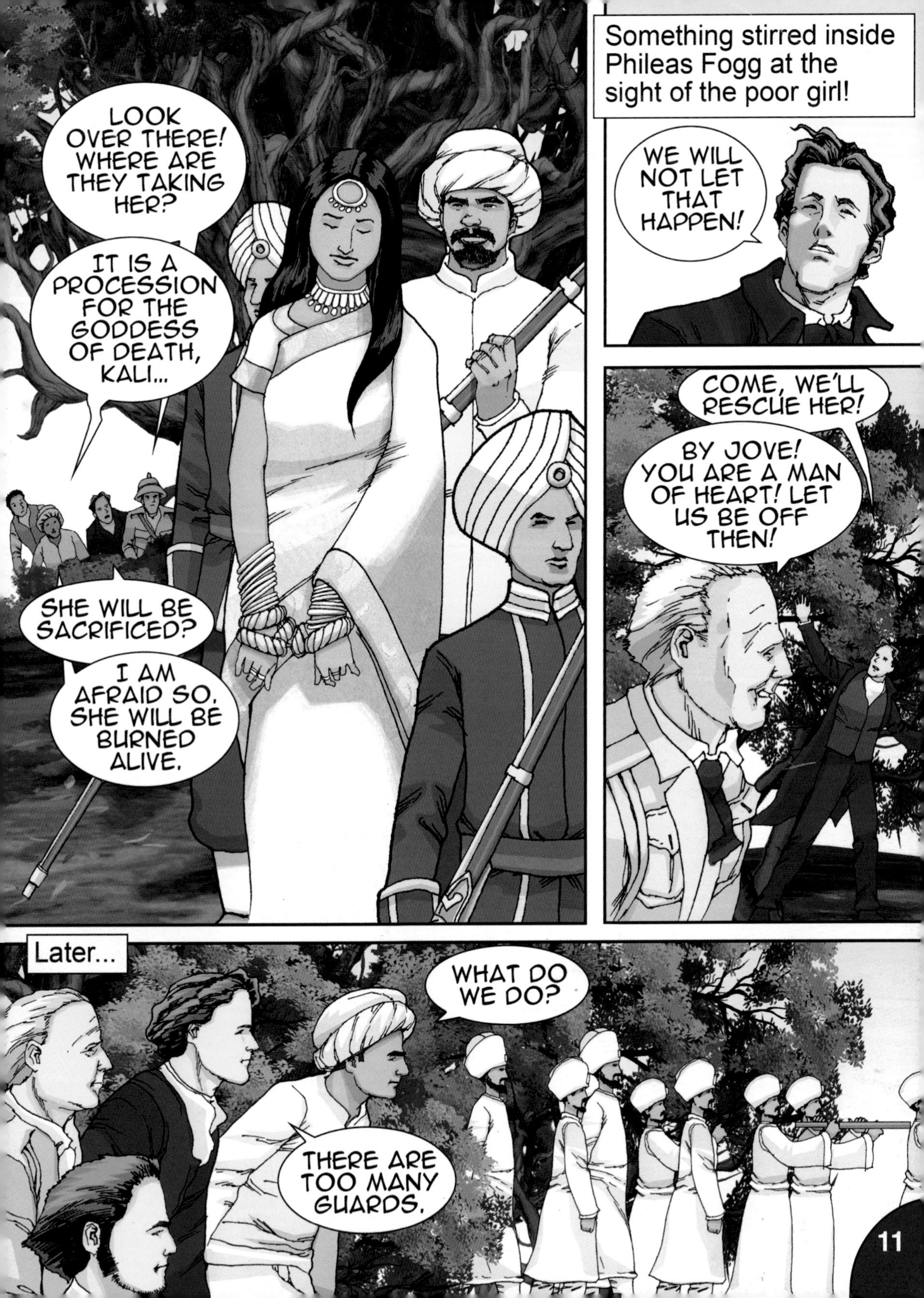
LOOK OVER THERE! WHERE ARE THEY TAKING HER?
IT IS A PROCESSION FOR THE GODDESS OF DEATH, KALI...
SHE WILL BE SACRIFICED?
I AM AFRAID SO. SHE WILL BE BURNED ALIVE.
Something stirred inside Phileas Fogg at the sight of the poor girl!
WE WILL NOT LET THAT HAPPEN!
COME, WE'LL RESCUE HER!
BY JOVE! YOU ARE A MAN OF HEART! LET US BE OFF THEN!
Later...
WHAT DO WE DO?
THERE ARE TOO MANY GUARDS.

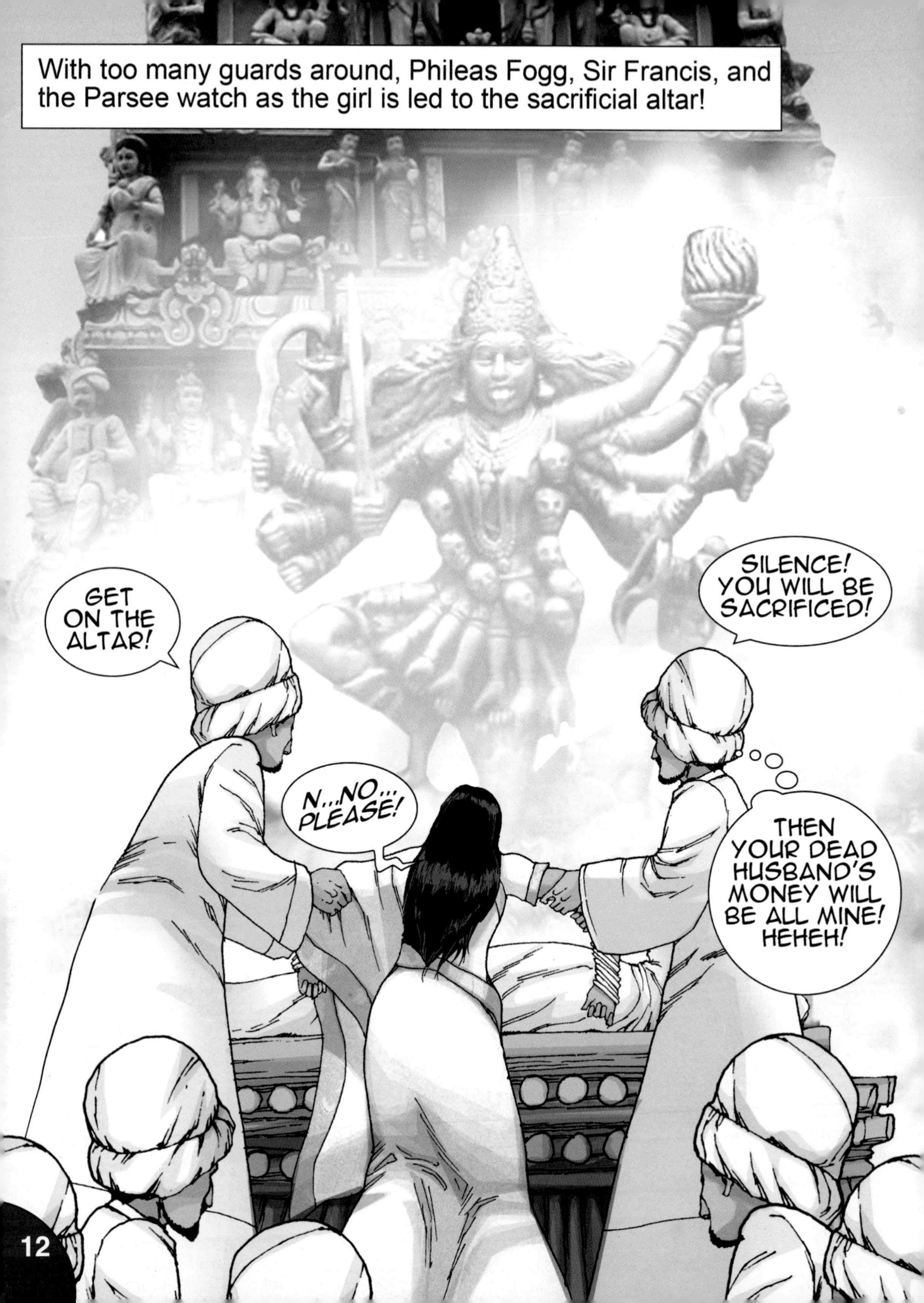
With too many guards around, Phileas Fogg, Sir Francis, and the Parsee watch as the girl is led to the sacrificial altar!
GET ON THE ALTAR!
SILENCE! YOU WILL BE SACRIFICED!
N...NO... PLEASE!
THEN YOUR DEAD HUSBAND'S MONEY WILL BE ALL MINE! HEHEH!

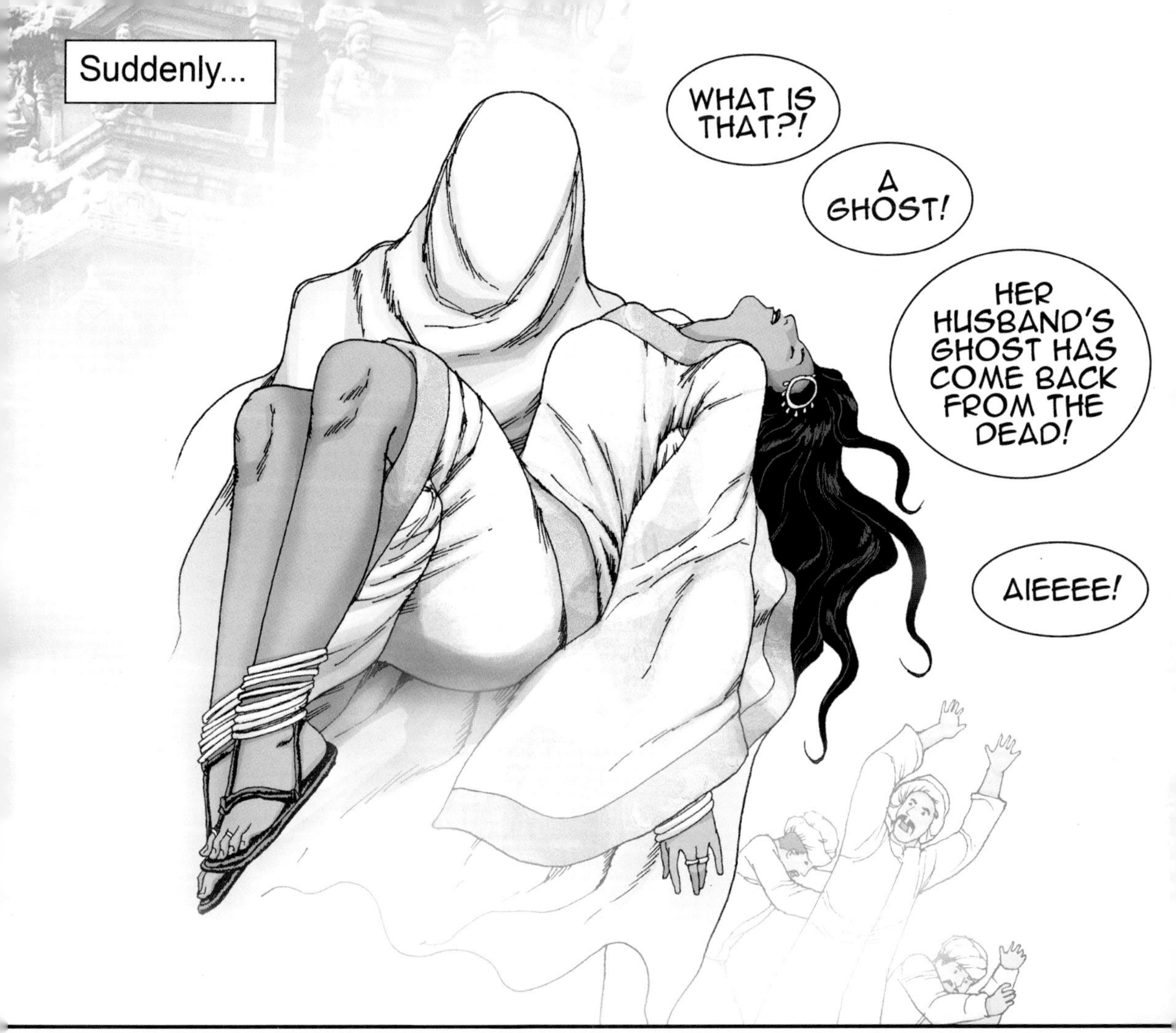
Suddenly...
WHAT IS THAT?!
A GHOST!
HER HUSBAND'S GHOST HAS COME BACK FROM THE DEAD!
AIEEEE!

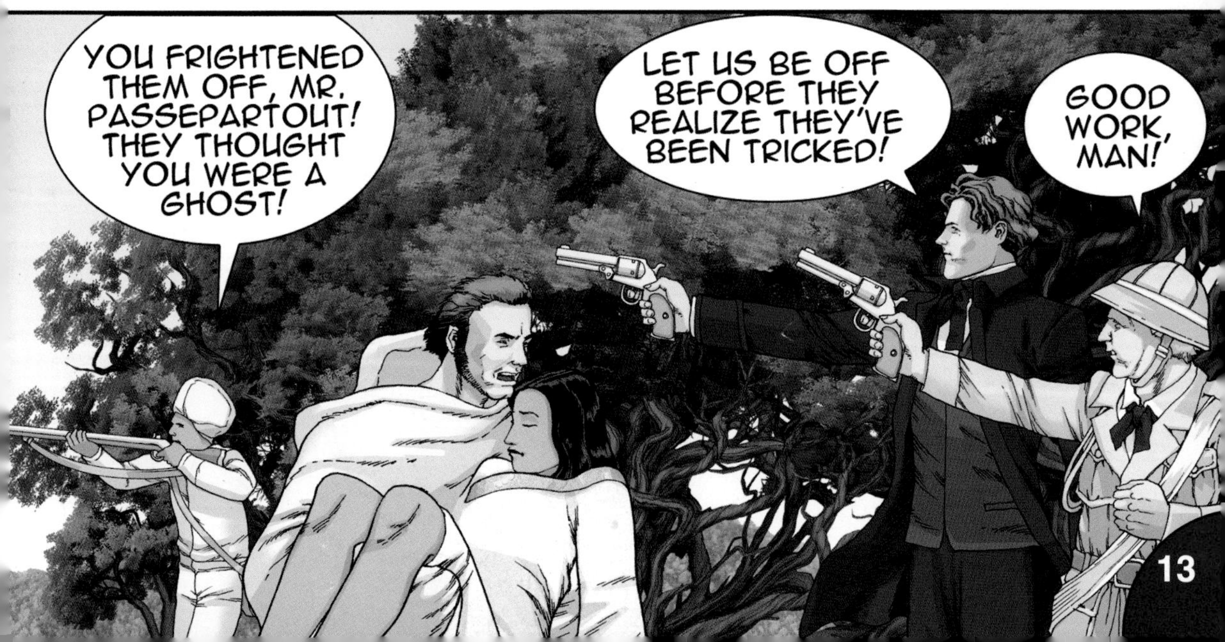
YOU FRIGHTENED THEM OFF, MR. PASSEPARTOUT! THEY THOUGHT YOU WERE A GHOST!
LET US BE OFF BEFORE THEY REALIZE THEY'VE BEEN TRICKED!
GOOD WORK, MAN!

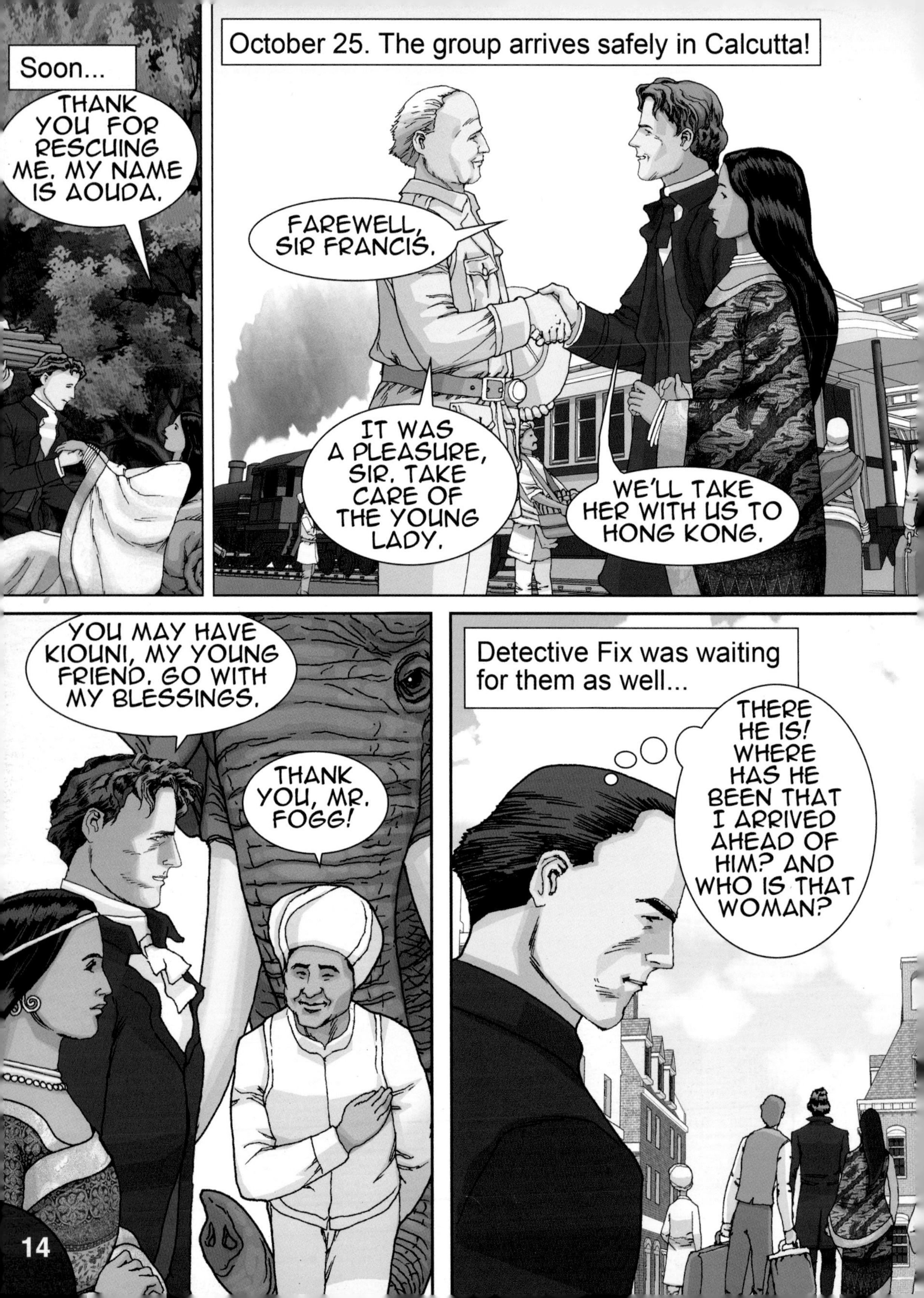

Soon...
THANK YOU FOR RESCUING ME. MY NAME IS AOUDA.
October 25. The group arrives safely in Calcutta!
FAREWELL, SIR FRANCIS.
IT WAS A PLEASURE, SIR. TAKE CARE OF THE YOUNG LADY.
WE'LL TAKE HER WITH US TO HONG KONG.
YOU MAY HAVE KIOUNI, MY YOUNG FRIEND. GO WITH MY BLESSINGS.
THANK YOU, MR. FOGG!
Detective Fix was waiting for them as well...
THERE HE IS! WHERE HAS HE BEEN THAT I ARRIVED AHEAD OF HIM? AND WHO IS THAT WOMAN?

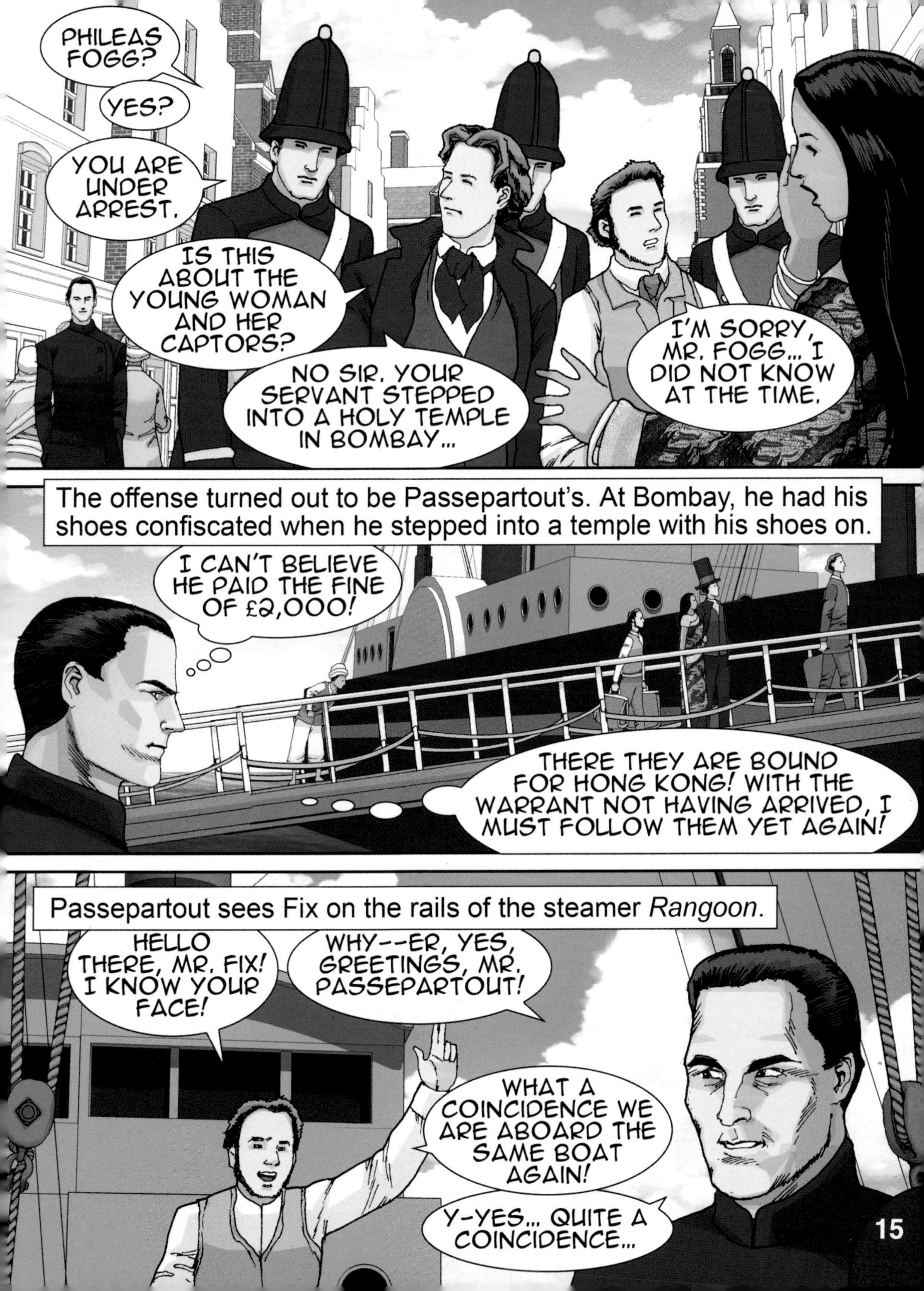
PHILEAS FOGG?
YES?
YOU ARE UNDER ARREST.
IS THIS ABOUT THE YOUNG WOMAN AND HER CAPTORS?
NO SIR. YOUR SERVANT STEPPED INTO A HOLY TEMPLE IN BOMBAY...
I'M SORRY, MR. FOGG... I DID NOT KNOW AT THE TIME.
The offense turned out to be Passepartout's. At Bombay, he had his shoes confiscated when he stepped into a temple with his shoes on.
I CAN'T BELIEVE HE PAID THE FINE OF £2,000!
THERE THEY ARE BOUND FOR HONG KONG! WITH THE WARRANT NOT HAVING ARRIVED, I MUST FOLLOW THEM YET AGAIN!
Passepartout sees Fix on the rails of the steamer *Rangoon*.
HELLO THERE, MR. FIX! I KNOW YOUR FACE!
WHY--ER, YES, GREETINGS, MR. PASSEPARTOUT!
WHAT A COINCIDENCE WE ARE ABOARD THE SAME BOAT AGAIN!
Y-YES... QUITE A COINCIDENCE...

Chapter 4 The Separation of Passepartout

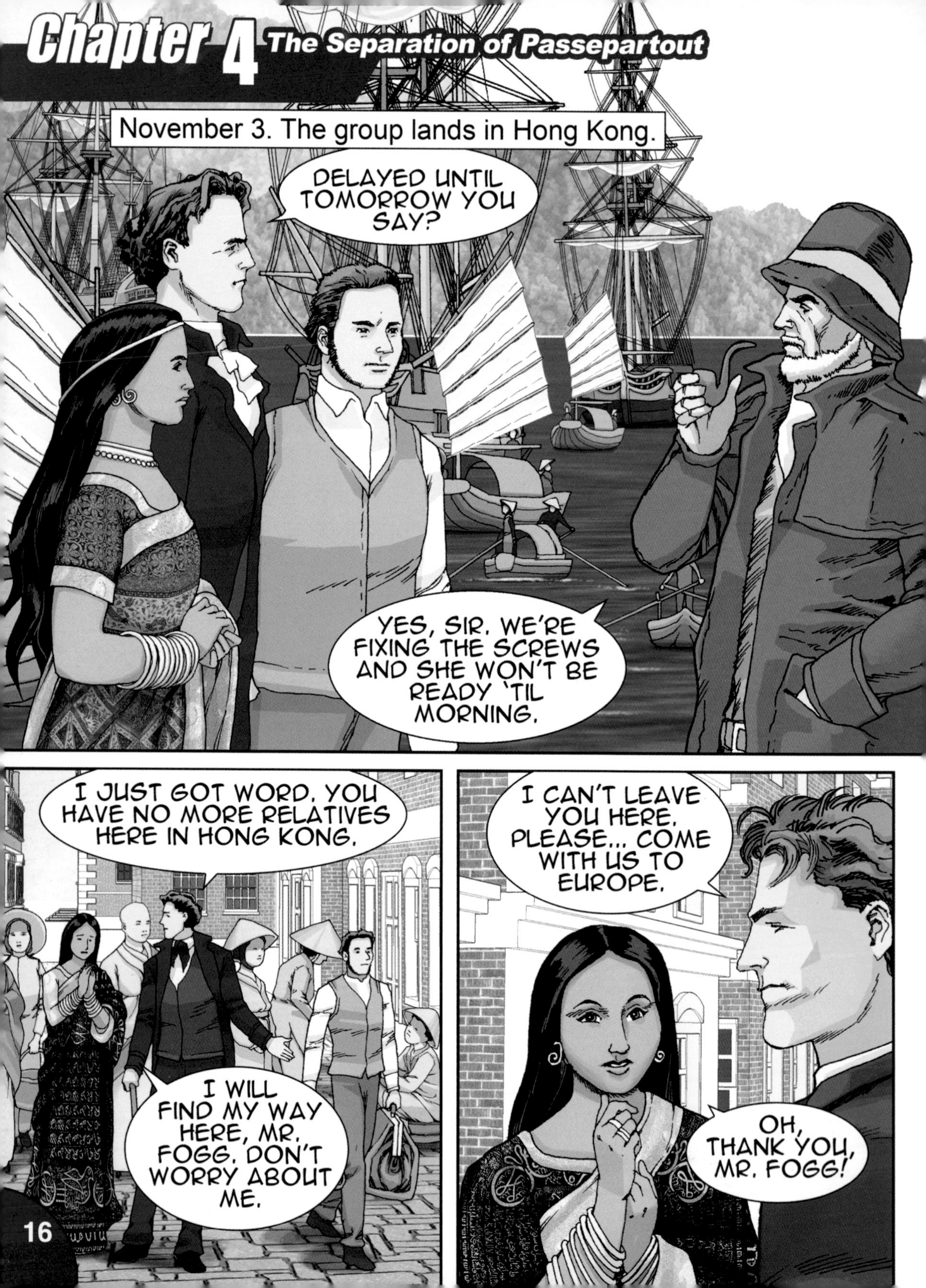
November 3. The group lands in Hong Kong.
DELAYED UNTIL TOMORROW YOU SAY?
YES, SIR. WE'RE FIXING THE SCREWS AND SHE WON'T BE READY 'TIL MORNING.
I JUST GOT WORD. YOU HAVE NO MORE RELATIVES HERE IN HONG KONG.
I WILL FIND MY WAY HERE, MR. FOGG. DON'T WORRY ABOUT ME.
I CAN'T LEAVE YOU HERE. PLEASE... COME WITH US TO EUROPE.
OH, THANK YOU, MR. FOGG!

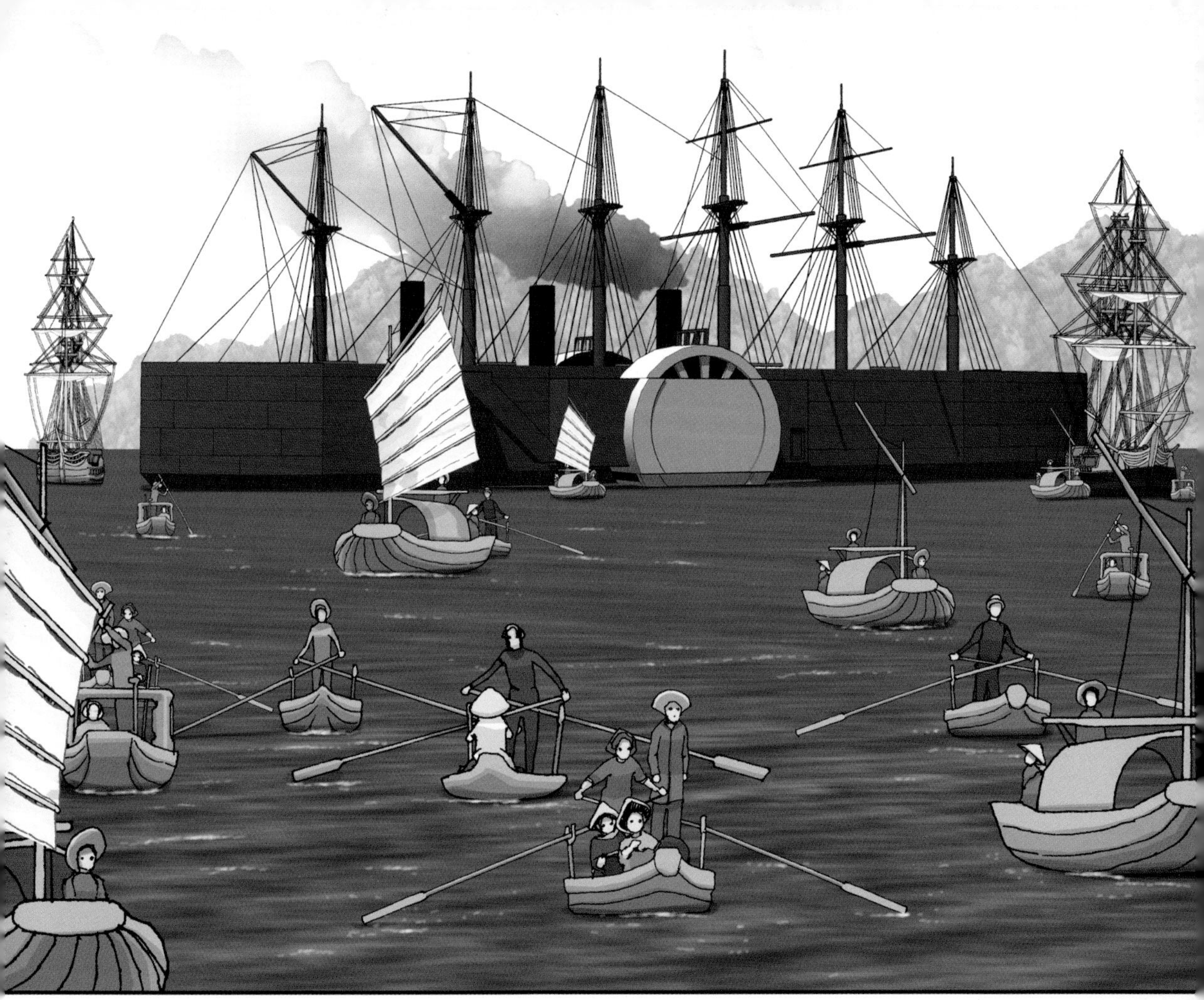

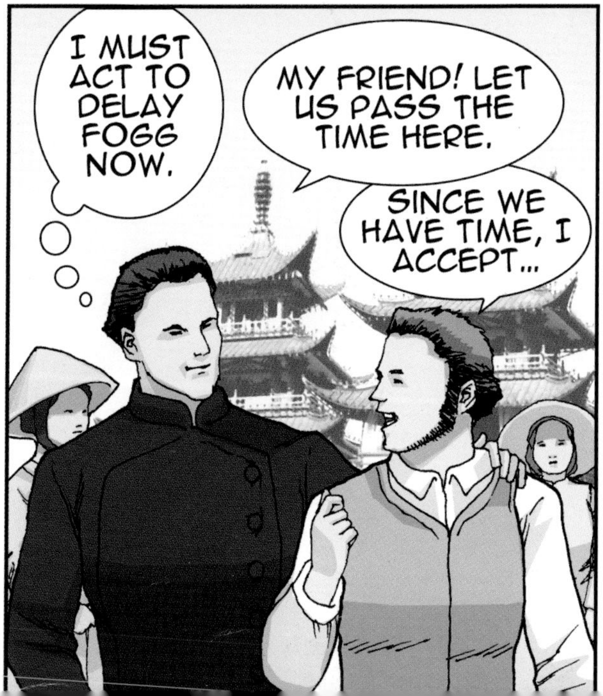
I MUST ACT TO DELAY FOGG NOW.
MY FRIEND! LET US PASS THE TIME HERE.
SINCE WE HAVE TIME, I ACCEPT...

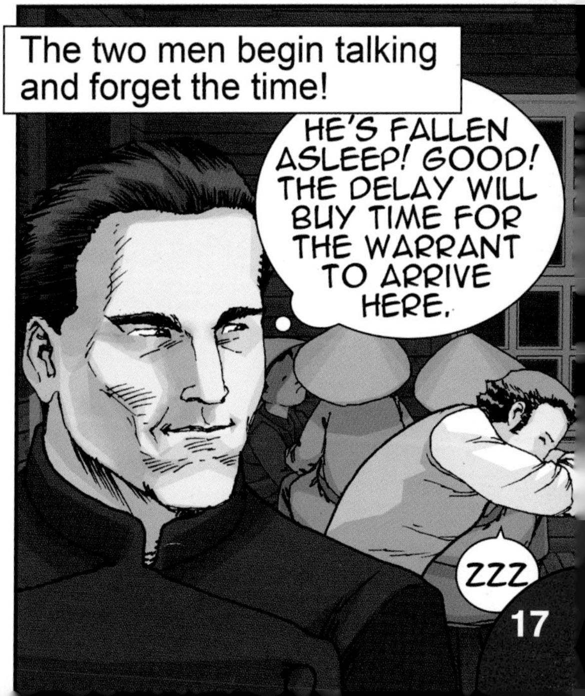
The two men begin talking and forget the time!
HE'S FALLEN ASLEEP! GOOD! THE DELAY WILL BUY TIME FOR THE WARRANT TO ARRIVE HERE.
ZZZ

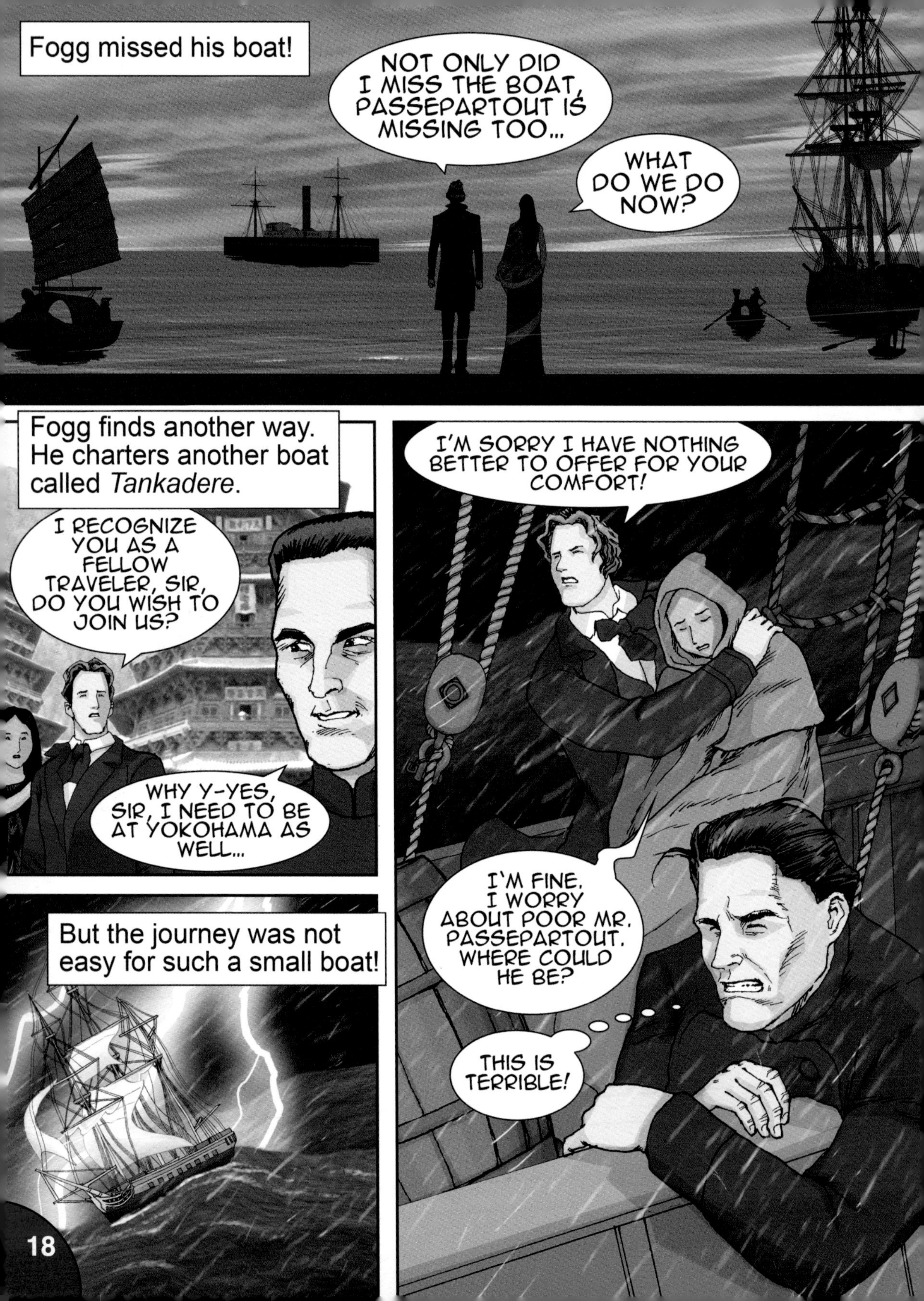
Fogg missed his boat!
NOT ONLY DID I MISS THE BOAT, PASSEPARTOUT IS MISSING TOO...
WHAT DO WE DO NOW?
Fogg finds another way. He charters another boat called *Tankadere*.
I RECOGNIZE YOU AS A FELLOW TRAVELER, SIR, DO YOU WISH TO JOIN US?
WHY Y-YES, SIR, I NEED TO BE AT YOKOHAMA AS WELL...
But the journey was not easy for such a small boat!
I'M SORRY I HAVE NOTHING BETTER TO OFFER FOR YOUR COMFORT!
I'M FINE. I WORRY ABOUT POOR MR. PASSEPARTOUT. WHERE COULD HE BE?
THIS IS TERRIBLE!

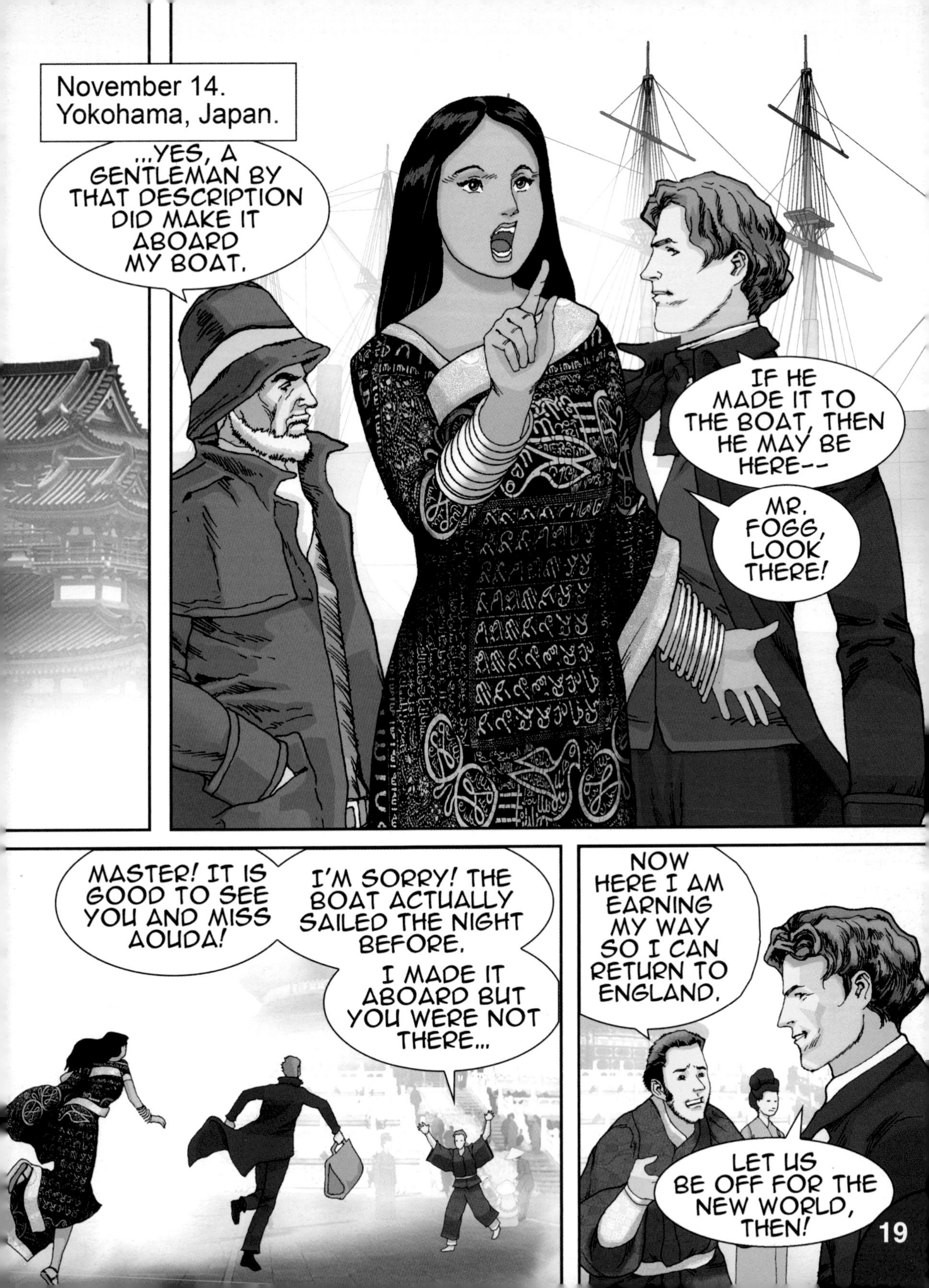
November 14. Yokohama, Japan.
...YES, A GENTLEMAN BY THAT DESCRIPTION DID MAKE IT ABOARD MY BOAT.
IF HE MADE IT TO THE BOAT, THEN HE MAY BE HERE--
MR. FOGG, LOOK THERE!
MASTER! IT IS GOOD TO SEE YOU AND MISS AOUDA!
I'M SORRY! THE BOAT ACTUALLY SAILED THE NIGHT BEFORE.
I MADE IT ABOARD BUT YOU WERE NOT THERE...
NOW HERE I AM EARNING MY WAY SO I CAN RETURN TO ENGLAND.
LET US BE OFF FOR THE NEW WORLD, THEN!

Chapter 5 To America!

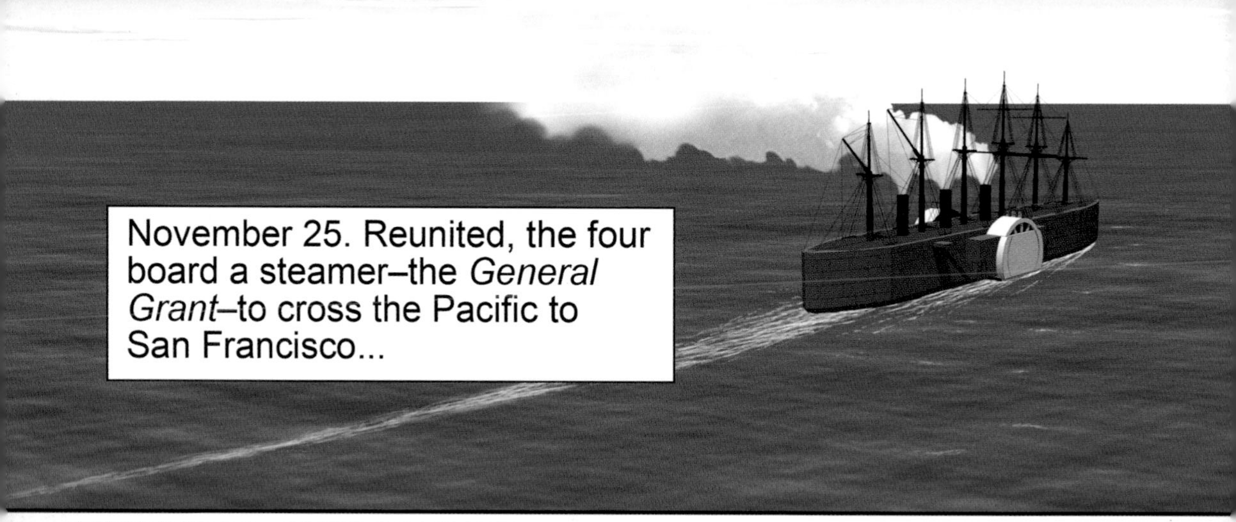
November 25. Reunited, the four board a steamer–the *General Grant*–to cross the Pacific to San Francisco...

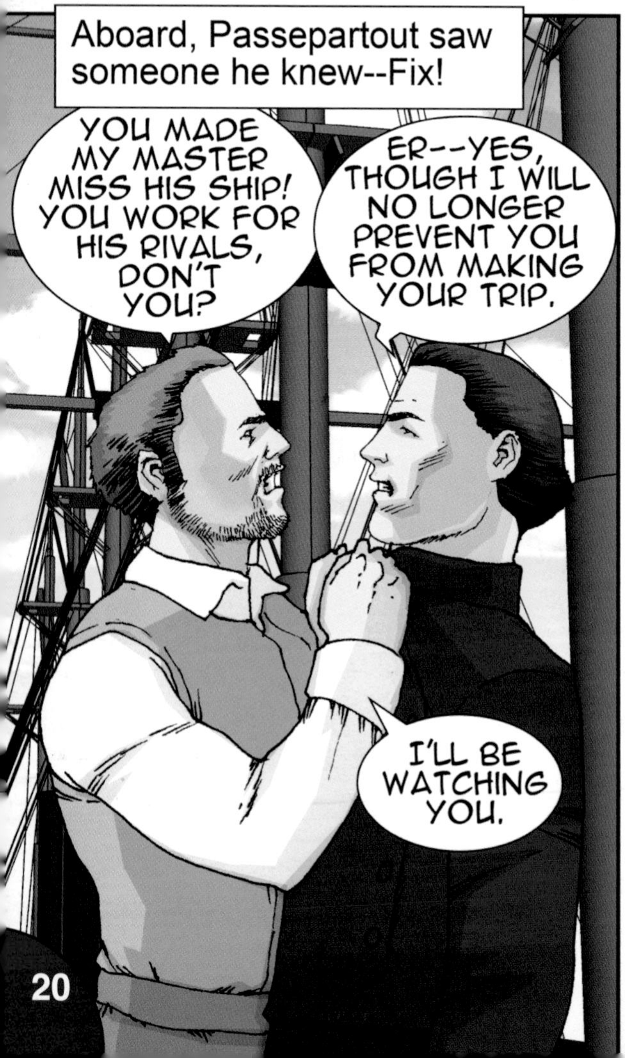
Aboard, Passepartout saw someone he knew--Fix!
YOU MADE MY MASTER MISS HIS SHIP! YOU WORK FOR HIS RIVALS, DON'T YOU?
ER--YES, THOUGH I WILL NO LONGER PREVENT YOU FROM MAKING YOUR TRIP.
I'LL BE WATCHING YOU.

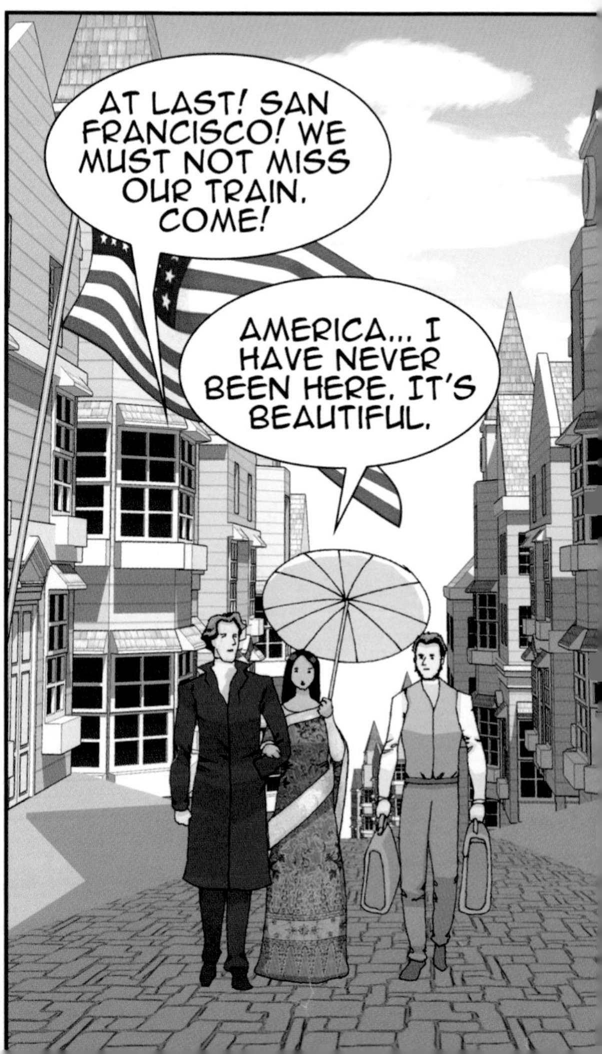
AT LAST! SAN FRANCISCO! WE MUST NOT MISS OUR TRAIN. COME!
AMERICA... I HAVE NEVER BEEN HERE. IT'S BEAUTIFUL.

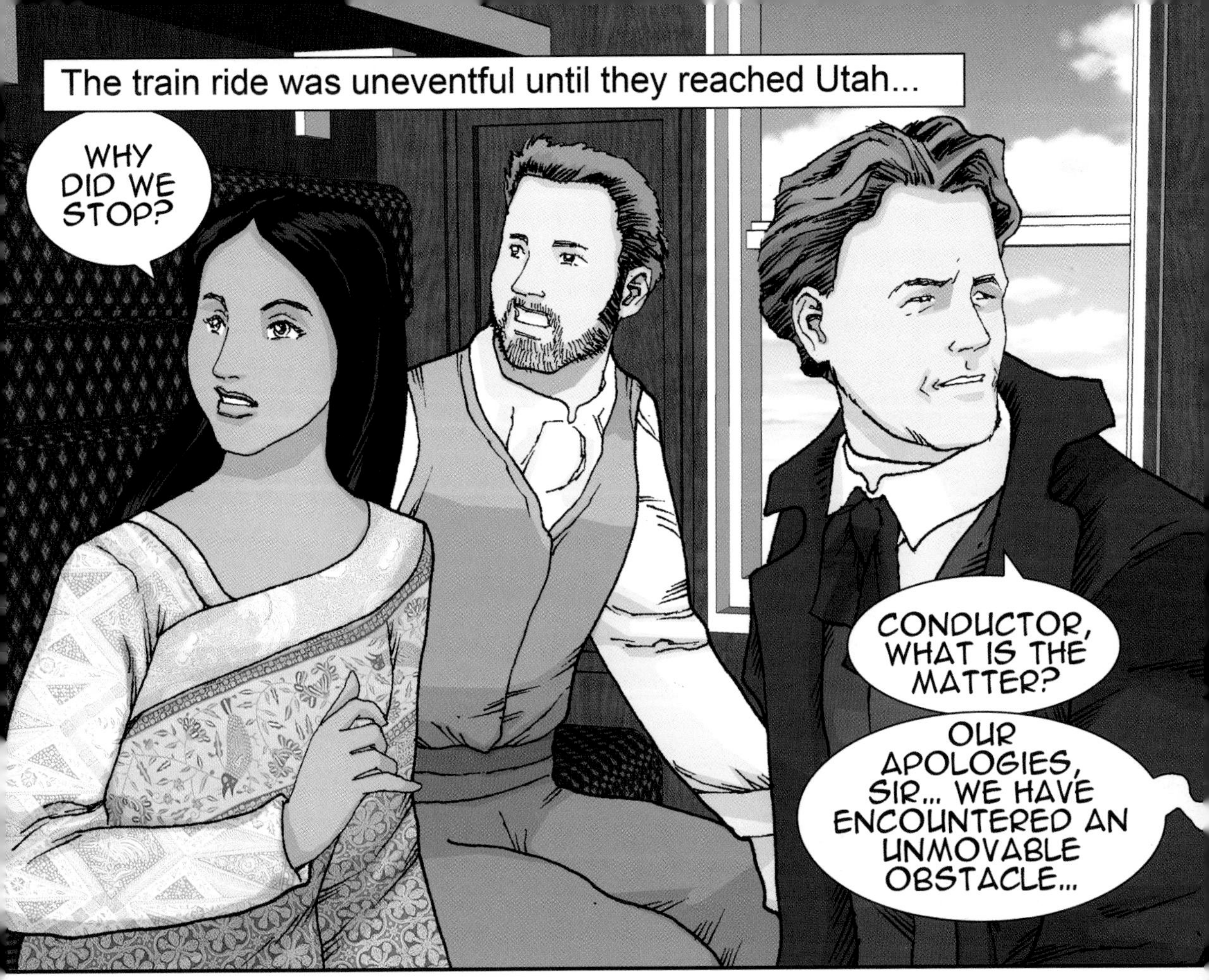
The train ride was uneventful until they reached Utah...
WHY DID WE STOP?
CONDUCTOR, WHAT IS THE MATTER?
OUR APOLOGIES, SIR... WE HAVE ENCOUNTERED AN UNMOVABLE OBSTACLE...

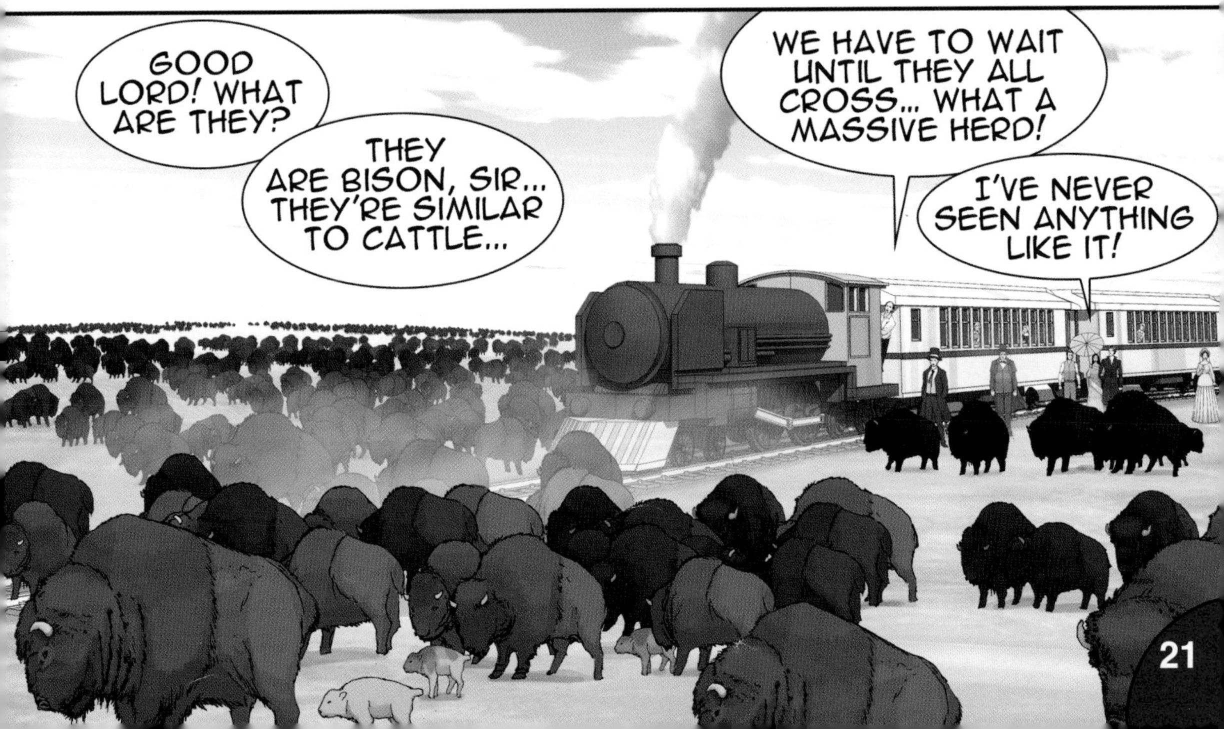
GOOD LORD! WHAT ARE THEY?
THEY ARE BISON, SIR... THEY'RE SIMILAR TO CATTLE...
WE HAVE TO WAIT UNTIL THEY ALL CROSS... WHAT A MASSIVE HERD!
I'VE NEVER SEEN ANYTHING LIKE IT!

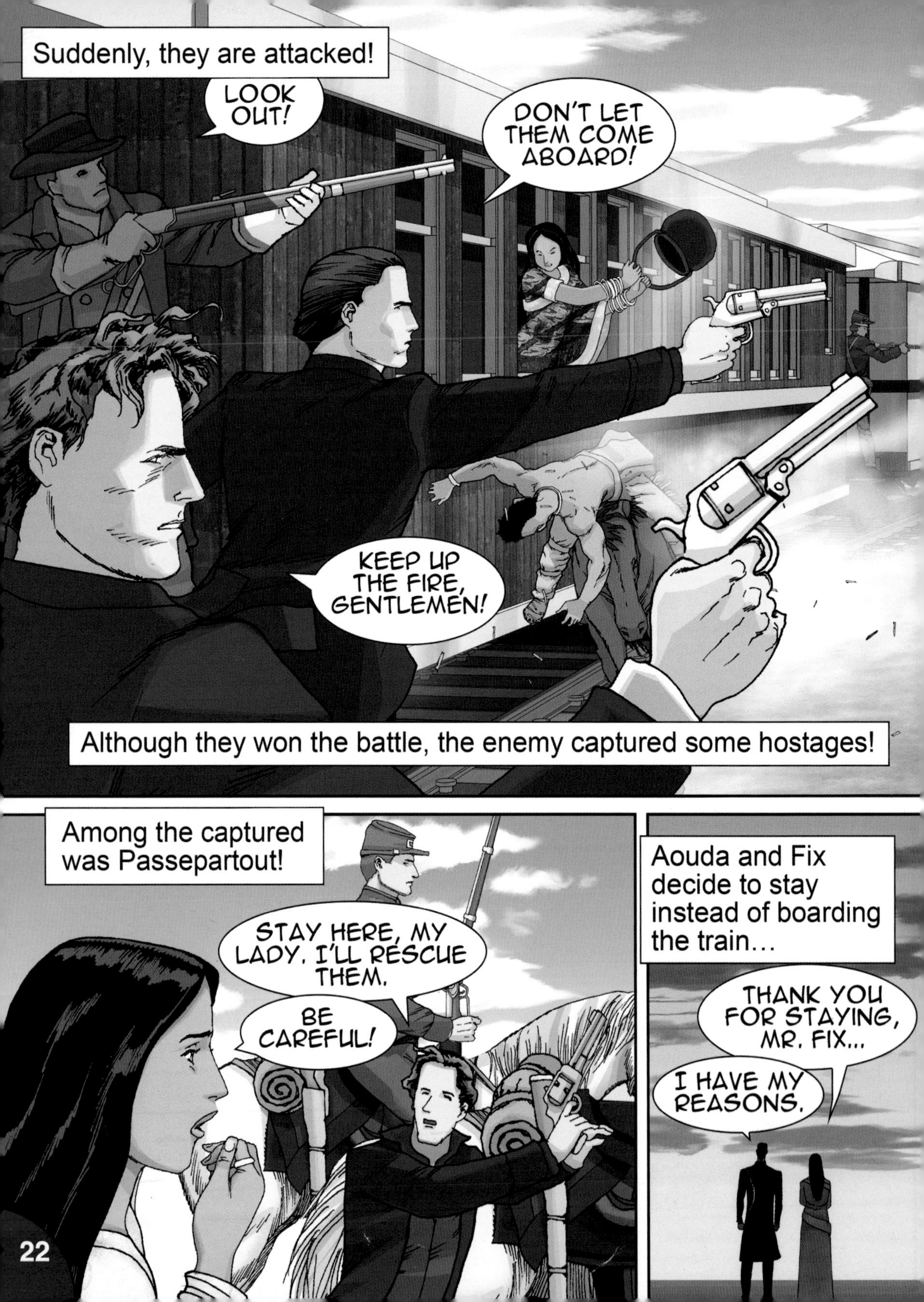
Suddenly, they are attacked!
LOOK OUT!
DON'T LET THEM COME ABOARD!
KEEP UP THE FIRE, GENTLEMEN!
Although they won the battle, the enemy captured some hostages!
Among the captured was Passepartout!
STAY HERE, MY LADY. I'LL RESCUE THEM.
BE CAREFUL!
Aouda and Fix decide to stay instead of boarding the train…
THANK YOU FOR STAYING, MR. FIX...
I HAVE MY REASONS.

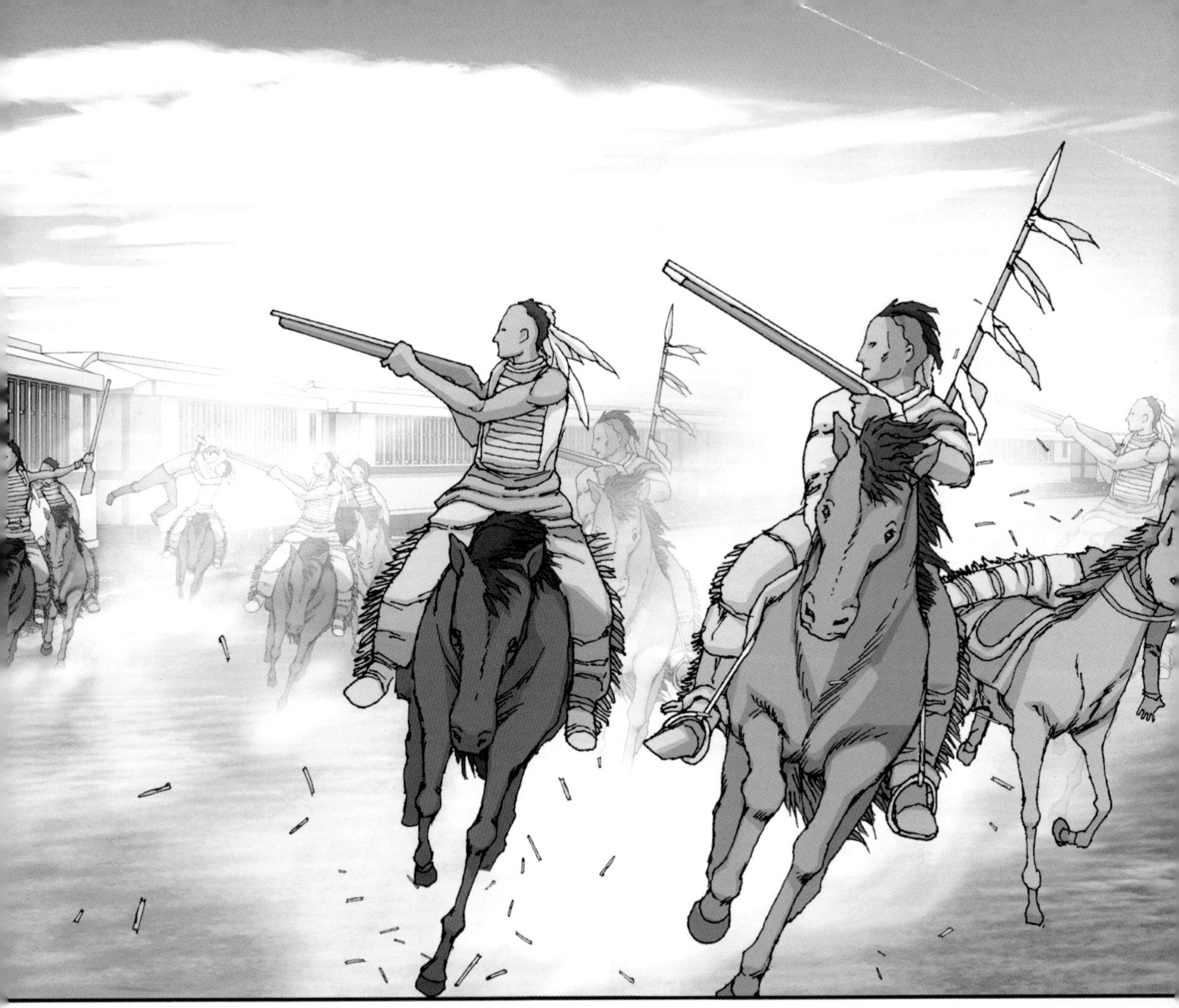

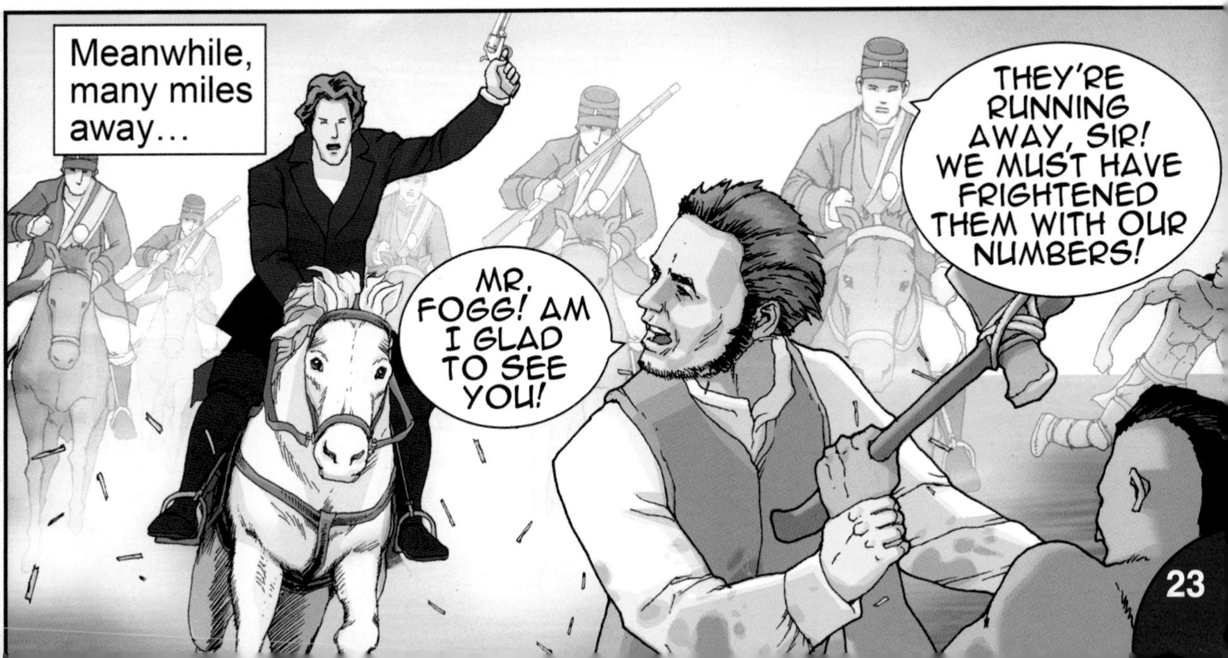
Meanwhile, many miles away…
THEY'RE RUNNING AWAY, SIR! WE MUST HAVE FRIGHTENED THEM WITH OUR NUMBERS!
MR. FOGG! AM I GLAD TO SEE YOU!

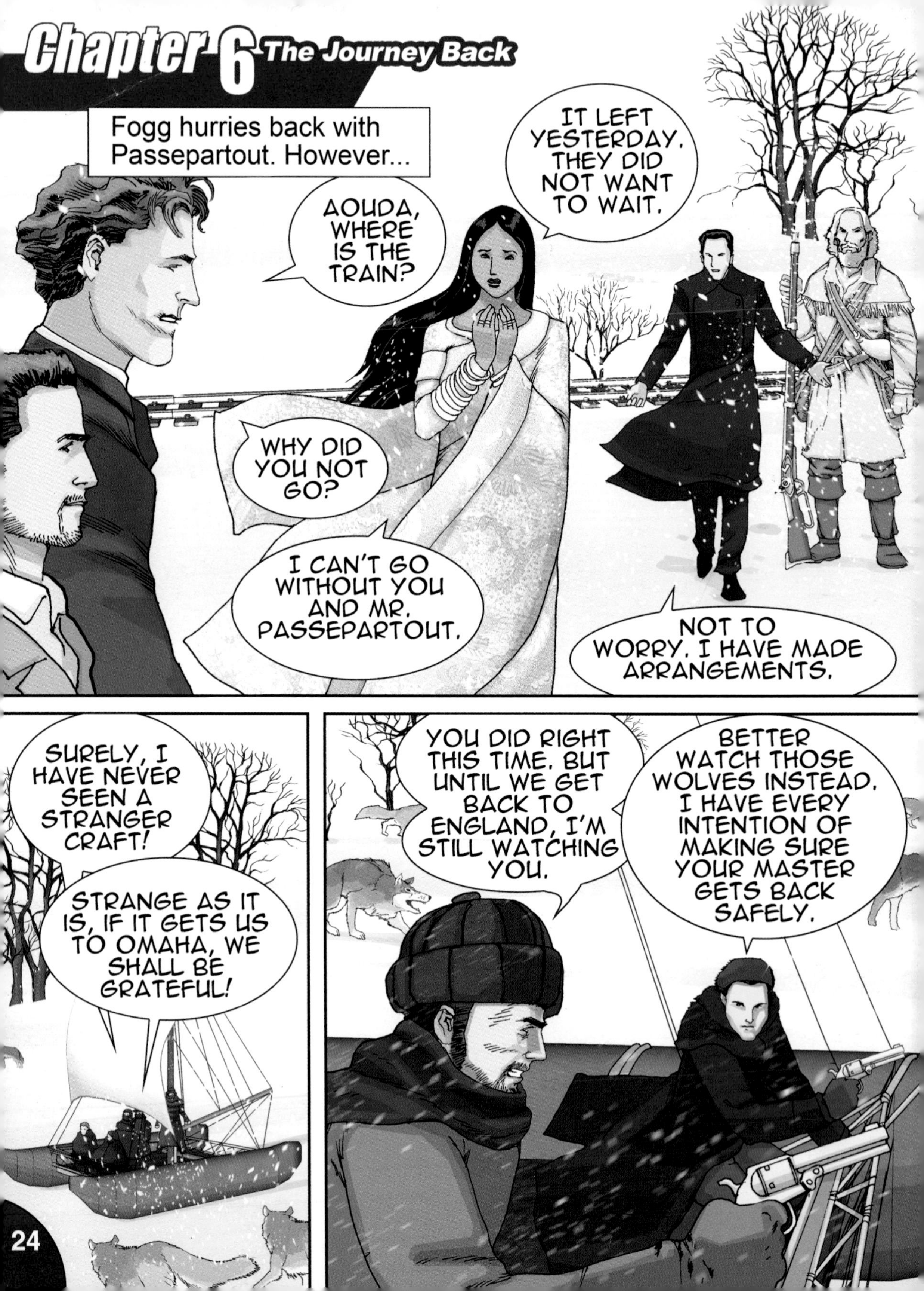
Chapter 6 The Journey Back
Fogg hurries back with Passepartout. However...
AOUDA, WHERE IS THE TRAIN?
IT LEFT YESTERDAY. THEY DID NOT WANT TO WAIT.
WHY DID YOU NOT GO?
I CAN'T GO WITHOUT YOU AND MR. PASSEPARTOUT.
NOT TO WORRY. I HAVE MADE ARRANGEMENTS.
SURELY, I HAVE NEVER SEEN A STRANGER CRAFT!
STRANGE AS IT IS, IF IT GETS US TO OMAHA, WE SHALL BE GRATEFUL!
YOU DID RIGHT THIS TIME. BUT UNTIL WE GET BACK TO ENGLAND, I'M STILL WATCHING YOU.
BETTER WATCH THOSE WOLVES INSTEAD. I HAVE EVERY INTENTION OF MAKING SURE YOUR MASTER GETS BACK SAFELY.

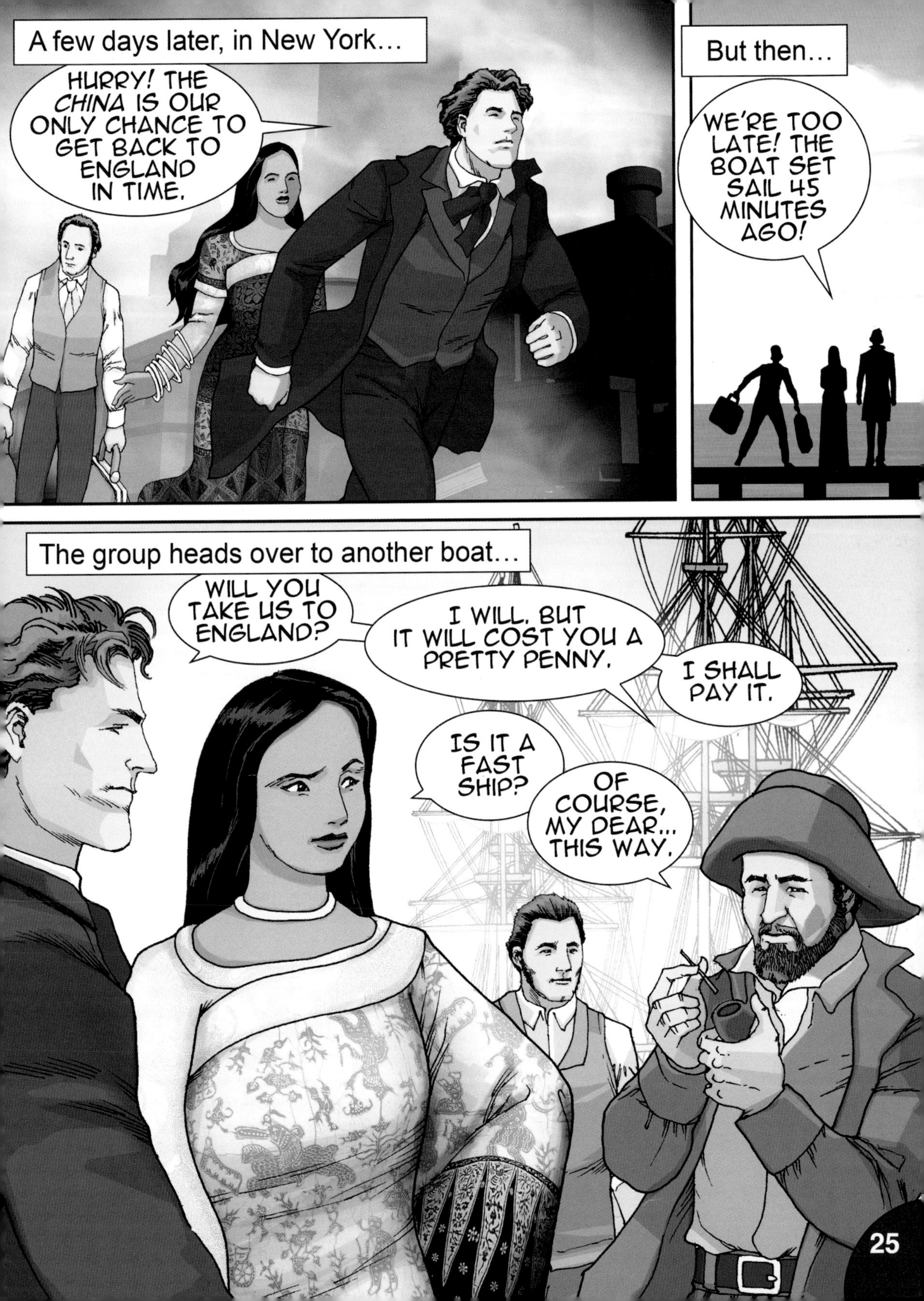
A few days later, in New York…
HURRY! THE *CHINA* IS OUR ONLY CHANCE TO GET BACK TO ENGLAND IN TIME.
But then…
WE'RE TOO LATE! THE BOAT SET SAIL 45 MINUTES AGO!
The group heads over to another boat…
WILL YOU TAKE US TO ENGLAND?
I WILL, BUT IT WILL COST YOU A PRETTY PENNY.
I SHALL PAY IT.
IS IT A FAST SHIP?
OF COURSE, MY DEAR... THIS WAY.

Chapter 7 The Race to England!

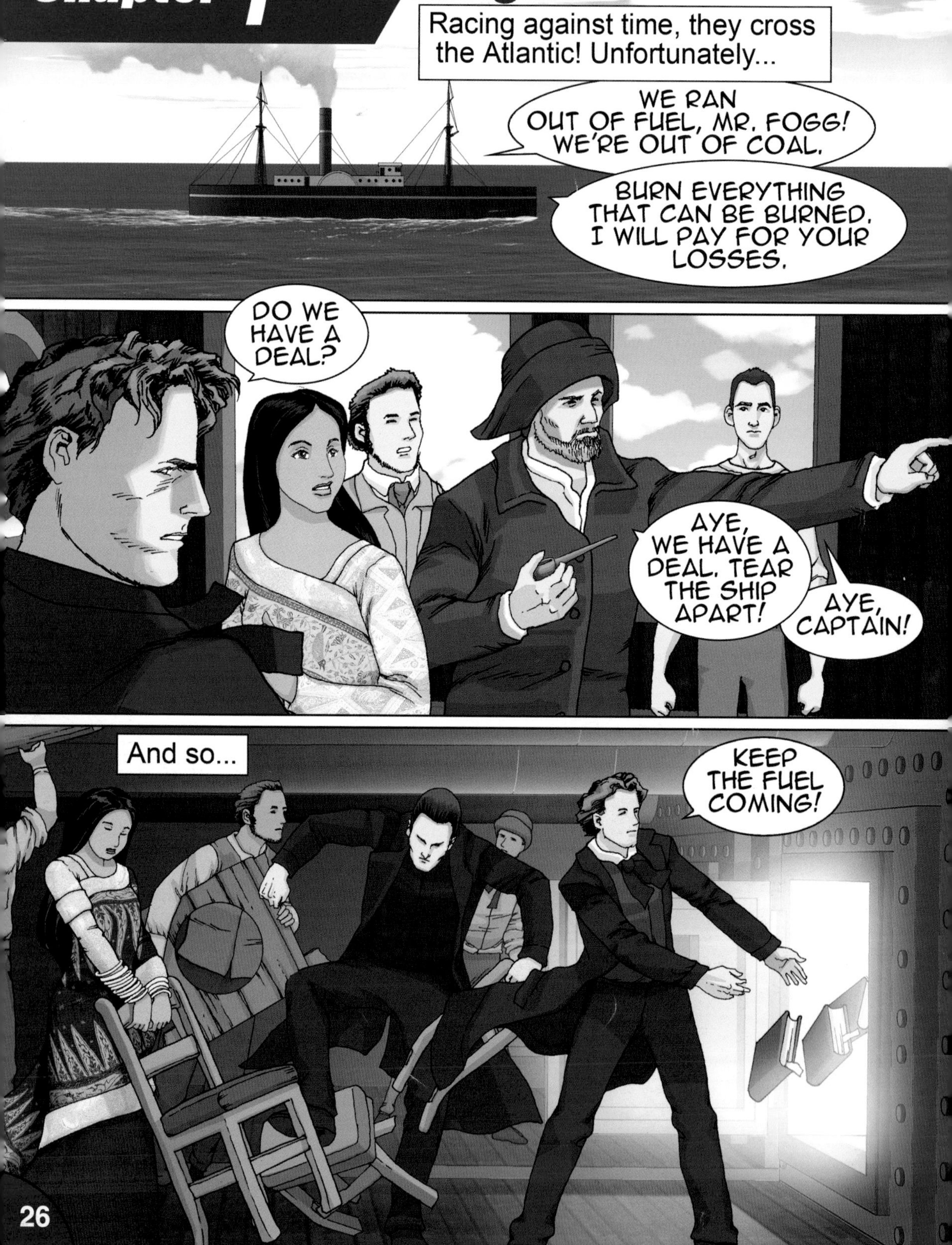
Racing against time, they cross the Atlantic! Unfortunately...
WE RAN OUT OF FUEL, MR. FOGG! WE'RE OUT OF COAL.
BURN EVERYTHING THAT CAN BE BURNED. I WILL PAY FOR YOUR LOSSES.
DO WE HAVE A DEAL?
AYE, WE HAVE A DEAL. TEAR THE SHIP APART!
AYE, CAPTAIN!
And so...
KEEP THE FUEL COMING!

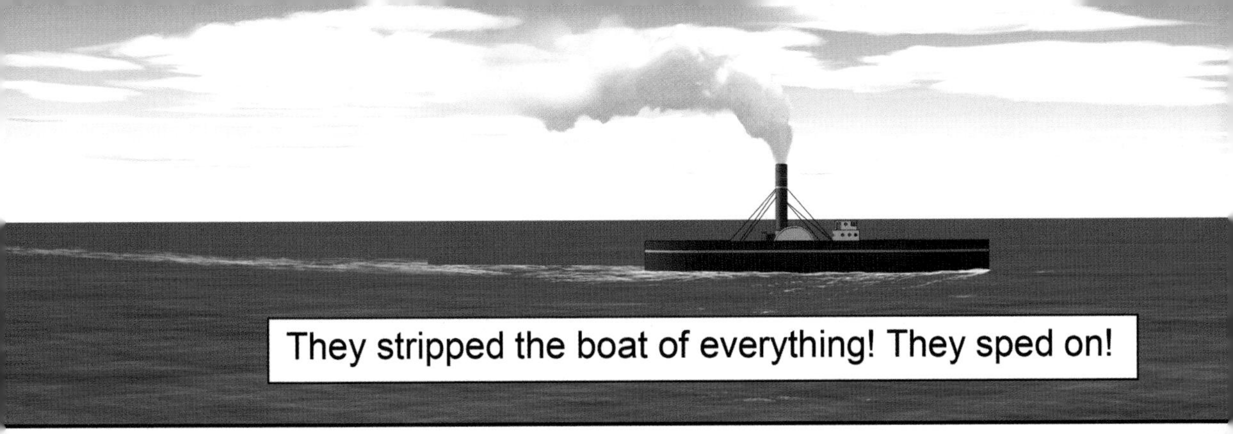
They stripped the boat of everything! They sped on!

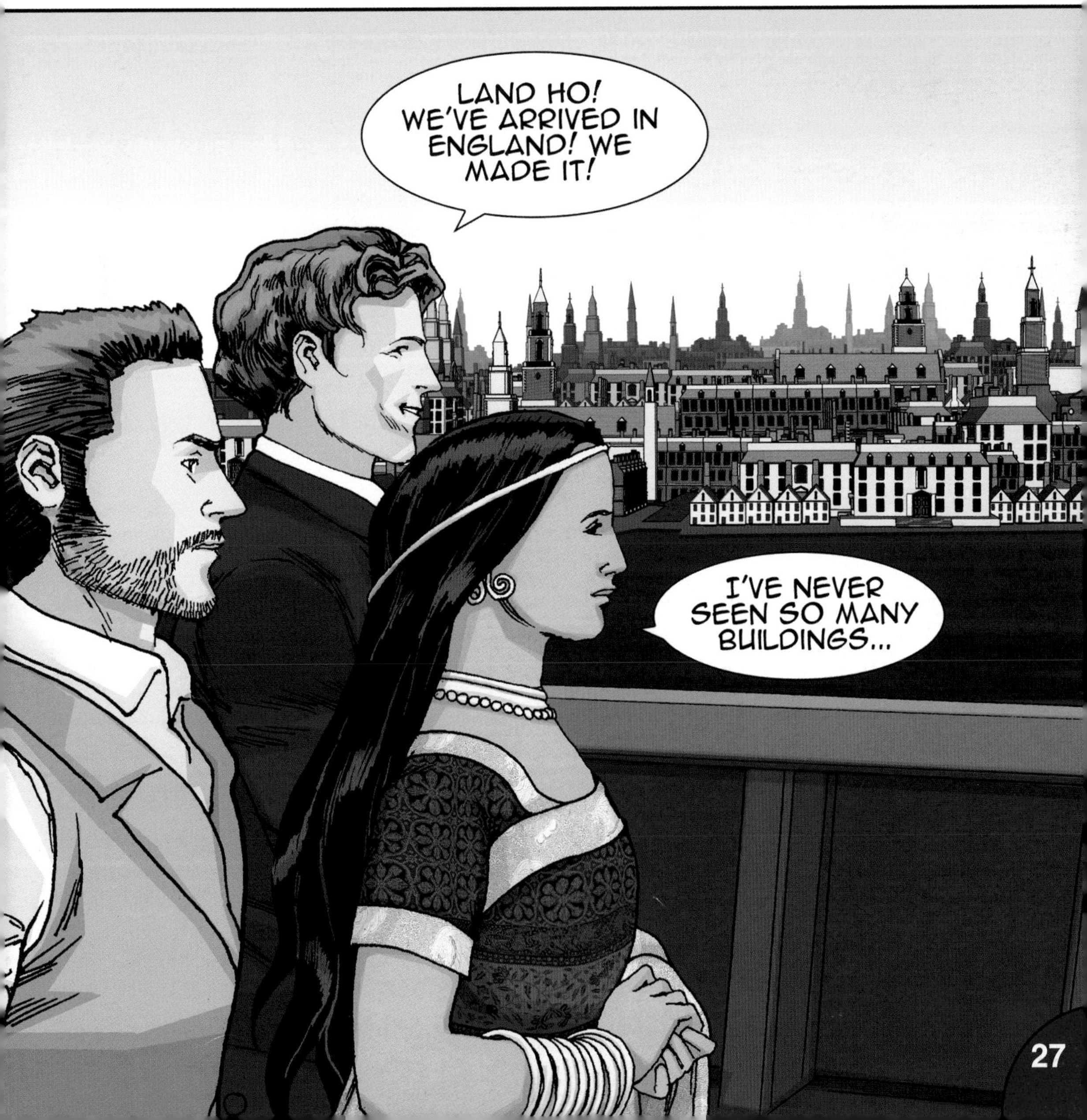
LAND HO! WE'VE ARRIVED IN ENGLAND! WE MADE IT!
I'VE NEVER SEEN SO MANY BUILDINGS...

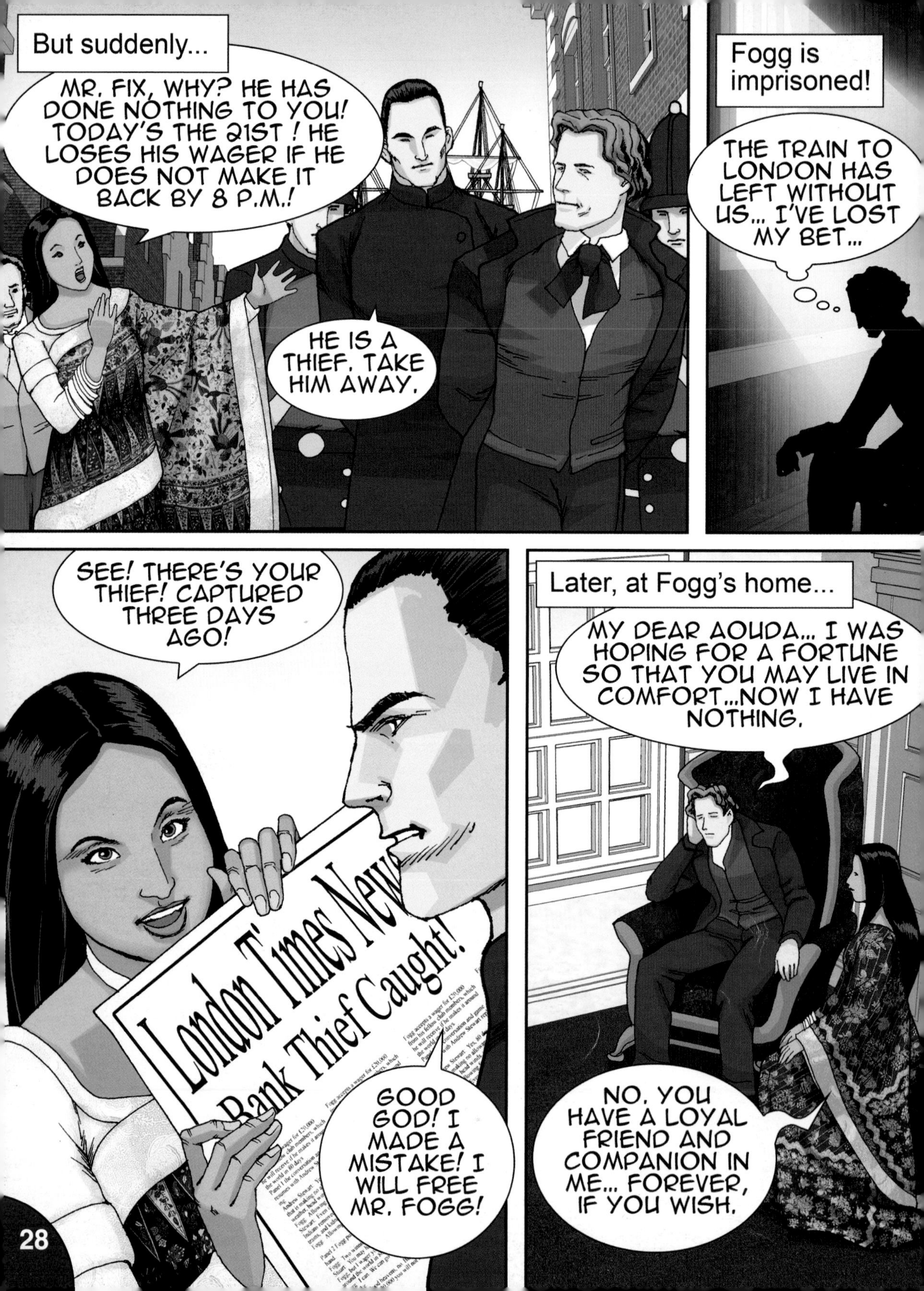
But suddenly...
MR. FIX, WHY? HE HAS DONE NOTHING TO YOU! TODAY'S THE 21ST ! HE LOSES HIS WAGER IF HE DOES NOT MAKE IT BACK BY 8 P.M.!
HE IS A THIEF. TAKE HIM AWAY.
Fogg is imprisoned!
THE TRAIN TO LONDON HAS LEFT WITHOUT US... I'VE LOST MY BET...
SEE! THERE'S YOUR THIEF! CAPTURED THREE DAYS AGO!
London Times New
Bank Thief Caught!
GOOD GOD! I MADE A MISTAKE! I WILL FREE MR. FOGG!
Later, at Fogg's home...
MY DEAR AOUDA... I WAS HOPING FOR A FORTUNE SO THAT YOU MAY LIVE IN COMFORT...NOW I HAVE NOTHING.
NO, YOU HAVE A LOYAL FRIEND AND COMPANION IN ME... FOREVER, IF YOU WISH.

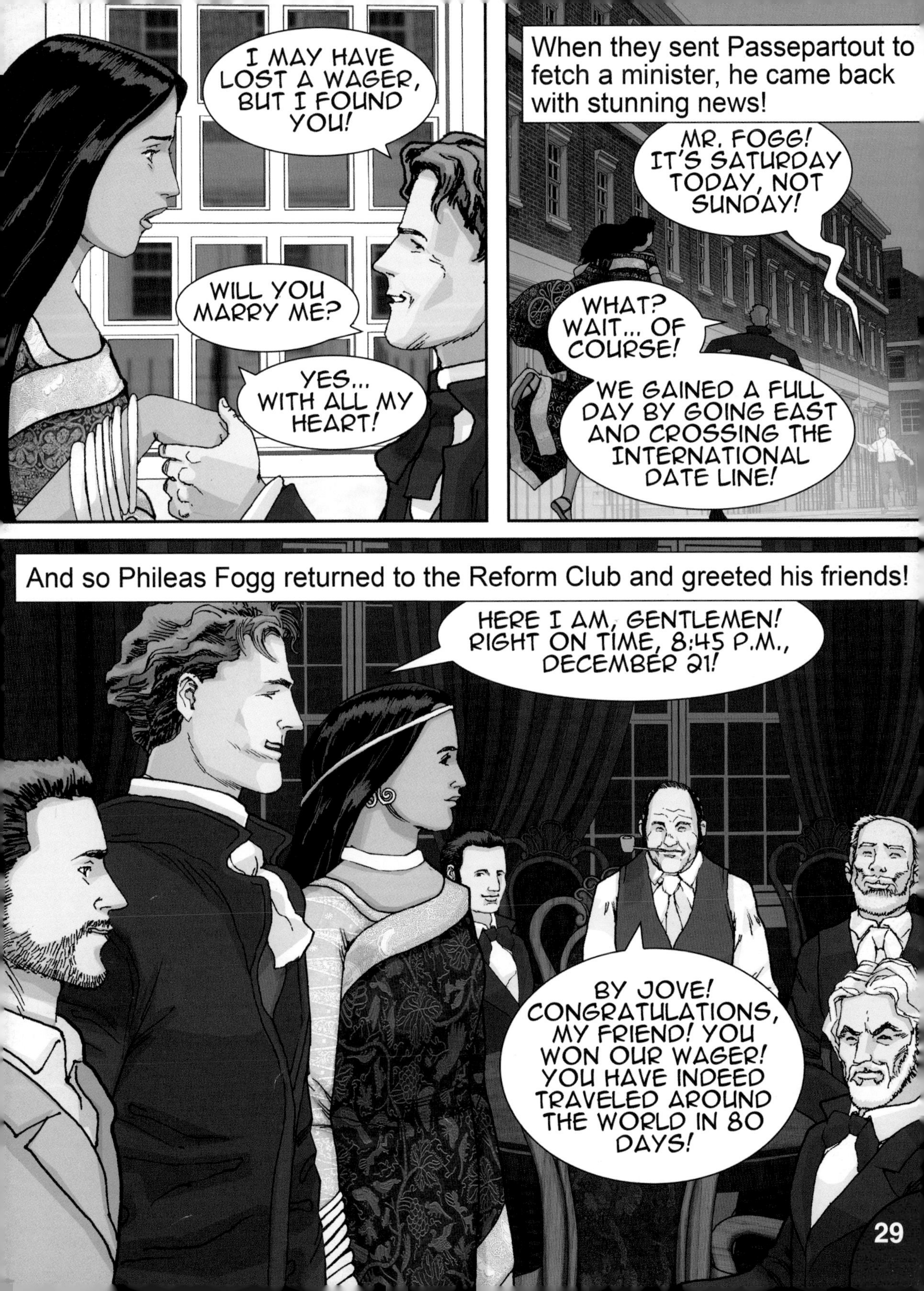
I MAY HAVE LOST A WAGER, BUT I FOUND YOU!
WILL YOU MARRY ME?
YES... WITH ALL MY HEART!
When they sent Passepartout to fetch a minister, he came back with stunning news!
MR. FOGG! IT'S SATURDAY TODAY, NOT SUNDAY!
WHAT? WAIT... OF COURSE!
WE GAINED A FULL DAY BY GOING EAST AND CROSSING THE INTERNATIONAL DATE LINE!
And so Phileas Fogg returned to the Reform Club and greeted his friends!
HERE I AM, GENTLEMEN! RIGHT ON TIME, 8:45 P.M., DECEMBER 21!
BY JOVE! CONGRATULATIONS, MY FRIEND! YOU WON OUR WAGER! YOU HAVE INDEED TRAVELED AROUND THE WORLD IN 80 DAYS!

About the Author

Jules Verne was born on February 8, 1828, in Nantes, France. His father was a lawyer in the port city. Jules always had a love of the sea and tried to run away. His father brought him home and later sent him to Paris to study law. Instead, Jules decided to become a writer.

In 1857, Verne married and became a stockbroker to support his family. He continued to write plays, short stories, and essays. It wasn't until 1863 that Verne quit his job and began writing full-time.

Verne met Jules Hetzel in 1863. Hetzel became Verne's publisher and mentor. He published Verne's first story in his magazine. Verne's work soon became popular. He cleverly included realistic details and explanations that supported his fantastic adventure tales.

Verne died on March 24, 1905, but his son Michel completed and published several of his manuscripts between 1905 and 1919. Today, Jules Verne is often remembered as the father of science fiction, and he remains an important influence on many writers.

Additional Works

Other works by Jules Verne include

Five Weeks in a Balloon (1863)
Journey to the Centre of the Earth (1867)
From the Earth to the Moon (1865)
Twenty Thousand Leagues Under the Sea (1870)
North Against South (1887)
Floating Island (1895)
The Golden Volcano (1906)
The Chase of the Golden Meteor (1908)

About the Adapter

Rod Espinosa is a graphic novel creator, writer, and illustrator. Espinosa was born in the Philippines in Manila. He graduated from the Don Bosco Technical College and Santo Tomas University.

Espinosa has worked in advertising, software entertainment, and film. Today, he lives in San Antonio, Texas, and produces stunning graphic novels including *Dinowars, Neotopia, Metadocs, Battle Girls,* and many others. His graphic novel *Courageous Princess* was nominated for an Eisner Award.

Glossary

Brahman - a person of the Hindu faith at the highest standing. Often a Brahman becomes a priest.

charter - to hire or rent a vehicle for personal use.

confiscate - to seize by authority.

consul - a government official sent to live in a foreign country and represent his or her government in the foreign country.

Parsee - the child of a Persian refugee who settled in Bombay.

Pound (£) - an English coin equal to 12 shillings. Twelve shillings weigh one pound.

visa - a stamp on a passport that allows a traveler to enter and leave a certain country.

Web Sites

To learn more about Jules Verne, visit ABDO Publishing Company on the World Wide Web at **www.abdopublishing.com.** Web sites about Verne are featured on our Book Links page. These links are routinely monitored and updated to provide the most current information available.